"Our child will not be illegitimate!

"We will get married," Morgan demanded.

This marriage was what Suzanna wanted more than anything. But not this way, not when Morgan was forced into it.

Morgan's expression changed as he looked at her. "Do you know what this means?"

"Yes, it means you will be forced to abdicate," Suzanna answered dully.

"Never!" he said angrily. "Our baby will have its rightful name."

"You're dreaming, Morgan. Even if your subjects accept me, we couldn't marry for at least four months. By that time I'll be visibly pregnant."

"We'll be married immediately, then, in a small private ceremony. Unless, of course, you don't want to see your life change overnight."

"How could I complain? What woman would object to becoming a queen?"

Dear Reader,

Welcome to Special Edition...where each month we offer six wonderfully emotional romances about people just like you—striving to find the perfect balance between life, career, family and, of course, love....

To start off, Susan Mallery shines with her thirtieth Silhouette novel, *Surprise Delivery*. In this not-to-be-missed THAT'S MY BABY! title, a very pregnant heroine is stuck in an elevator with a charming stranger—and is about to give birth!

Love proves to be the greatest adventure of all in *Hunter's Pride* by Lindsay McKenna. In the continuation of her enthralling MORGAN'S MERCENARIES: THE HUNTERS series, fiercely proud Devlin Hunter is teamed up with a feisty beauty who challenges him at every turn. And don't miss the wonderful romance between a harried single dad and a spirited virgin in *The Home Love Built* by Christine Flynn.

Next, a compassionate paralegal reunites a brooding cop with his twin sons in *The Fatherhood Factor*—book three in Diana Whitney's heartwarming FOR THE CHILDREN series. Then a lovely newcomer befriends her neighbor's little boy and breaks through to the lad's guarded dad in *My Child, Our Child* by *New York Times* bestselling author Patricia Hagan.

Finally this month, Tracy Sinclair pens *The Bachelor King,* a regally romantic tale about a powerful king who marries a "pregnant" American beauty, only to receive the royal shock of his life!

I hope you enjoy these six unforgettable romances created *by* women like you, *for* women like you!

Sincerely,

Karen Taylor Richman
Senior Editor

Please address questions and book requests to:
Silhouette Reader Service
U.S.: 3010 Walden Ave., P.O. Box 1325, Buffalo, NY 14269
Canadian: P.O. Box 609, Fort Erie, Ont. L2A 5X3

TRACY SINCLAIR

THE BACHELOR KING

Silhouette ®

SPECIAL ▼ **EDITION** ®

Published by Silhouette Books

America's Publisher of Contemporary Romance

SILHOUETTE BOOKS

ISBN 0-373-24278-6

THE BACHELOR KING

Visit us at www.romance.net

Printed in U.S.A.

TRACY SINCLAIR

began her career as a photojournalist for national magazines and newspapers. Extensive travel all over the world has provided this California resident with countless fascinating experiences, settings and acquaintances to draw on in plotting her romances. After writing over fifty novels for Silhouette, she still has stories she can't wait to tell.

Mr. and Mrs. Bentley
of Philadelphia, Pennsylvania,
are honored to announce
the sudden marriage of
their only daughter,
Miss Suzanna,
to
His Highness Morgan de Souverain,
King of Monrovia.
The couple were married in
a small ceremony
in the royal garden
at Beaumaire Castle, Monrovia.
In lieu of silver and crystal,
His and Her Majesty request
baby blankets, rattles and booties.

Chapter One

Suzanna Bentley had been working at Beaumaire Castle for a week, and she still hadn't gotten a glimpse of the king.

It would have been exciting. Morgan de Souverain was the most eligible royal in Europe. He was rich, handsome and possessed an imposing lineage. Even without all the advantages of wealth and power, he was definitely a hunk, judging by his photographs in newspapers and magazines. She'd always been attracted to dark-haired men with the intelligence and sense of humor King Morgan was reported to have.

But the real thrill for Suzanna was landing a job in Monrovia, a picturesque little country on the Adriatic. She'd been hired to restore the paintings in the royal art collection that had been damaged in a recent fire.

She was concentrating on a particularly tricky section of a priceless masterpiece when someone entered her studio and came over to stand in back of her.

"Is it customary to use such a small paintbrush?" a deep male voice asked. "Isn't that rather unusual?"

"No. I'm removing the soot caused by the fire."

"Wouldn't a cloth or a sponge be faster?"

"I'm not looking for speed. I'm more interested in the safety of the paint underneath."

"But if you…"

Suzanna gritted her teeth. "This takes a lot of concentration. I don't want to sound rude, but don't you have anything better to do than stand around pestering people who are working?"

"That's the advantage of being king." Morgan de Souverain gave a rich, male chuckle. "You can be a nuisance and get away with it."

Suzanna turned her head swiftly and suppressed a groan. "I'm really sorry, Your Highness," she mumbled. "I didn't know… I mean, I was at a difficult point, but I shouldn't have…"

"No, you were perfectly right," he said pleasantly. "It was disruptive to barge in on you like this."

"It's your castle and your art collection." She pulled off her baseball cap hurriedly in an attempt to look more presentable, but she doubted if it was an improvement. The jeans and sweatshirt she was wearing looked shabby compared to the king's immaculate white linen slacks and blue silk sport shirt. Her hair was disheveled, too, from being stuffed under the cap. She couldn't even comb it into some semblance of order with her fingers. They were sticky with solvent.

Morgan didn't find anything wrong with her. His face wore a wholly male look as he gazed at her delicate features. The woman was incredibly sexy! With that glorious mane of tousled hair framing her flushed cheeks and softly parted lips, she looked as if she'd just made love—and enjoyed it.

Suzanna was too rattled to notice the expression on his face. She took a deep breath and reminded herself that she was a well-regarded professional, hired to do an important job.

"Would you like a progress report?" she asked after regaining her poise. "I have encouraging news for you. Many of the pictures weren't damaged as badly as we at first feared."

"That *is* good news," he answered, with no sign of the erotic images she'd inspired. "Fortunately, the fire was discovered almost immediately and confined to a single wing of the castle. I'm told the restoration will take weeks, however, perhaps even longer." He slanted a glance at her. "Will you be able to remain here that long? I was told you're one of the busiest professionals in the art world."

"It won't be a problem," she assured him. "I had cleared my calendar because I intended to take a vacation—which I gladly postponed for a chance like this. I can stay until the job is done."

"That's good. I'd prefer that the restoration process be handled by one person, from start to finish." He glanced around the cluttered studio. "Doesn't it get rather lonely working here all by yourself?"

"No, I prefer it. My work takes a lot of concentration. With a studio all to myself, nobody bothers me."

"Except me." His eyes danced mischievously.

"I always seem to say the wrong thing to you." She sighed. "But it's just because I'm nervous. I've never met a king before."

He looked at her with a raised eyebrow. "Somehow, I don't think a mere male could make you nervous."

"You aren't like other men."

"Trust me, I am," he answered in a honeyed voice.

Did he really believe that? The average man didn't have the taut body of a champion athlete, or the square jaw and rugged features that drew women like a magnet.

Morgan de Souverain was the darling of the jet set and the object of daydreams by females from sixteen to sixty, judging by the articles written about him. He played hard, but he worked equally hard. Monrovia was one of the most stable countries on the continent, monarchy or republic.

Suzanna ignored his suggestive remark and said, "Would you like me to explain what I'm doing?"

He sat down and she briefly described different methods of cleaning and restoration, expecting him to be polite, yet bored. But the king surprised her. He knew a great deal about the process. Like how many coats of varnish an old painting might have, and the best way to remove them.

"How do you know things like that?" she asked with renewed respect.

"I make it my business to know about everything that goes on in my kingdom, and especially here in the castle. Does that surprise you? I hope you didn't share the belief, common in some quarters, that I'm simply a playboy monarch.''

"No, of course not!"

"Are you sure?" He smiled. "I'm very good at telling when people are lying to me."

"You mean you're a mind reader?" she asked lightly.

"Something like that. In my position, people tell me what they think I want to hear. You learn to separate truth from fiction."

"I suppose when you're a king, nobody wants to bring you bad news. But I can think of worse things than having everyone tell you how wonderful you are."

"You must hear that quite often." His expression changed as his tawny eyes swept over her discreetly.

"As you just said, people often pay insincere compliments," she said dismissively. "The only time I can be sure they're sincere is when they compliment my work." She gave an embarrassed little laugh. "That sounds immodest, doesn't it?"

"Not when it's the truth. I had my people search for the best restorer in the business, and you were highly recommended by several curators." He gave her a curious look. "You seem very young to have achieved such prominence in your field."

"I had to overcome some prejudice because of my age, but I didn't let it bother me. You probably experienced the same skepticism when you took over the throne."

He shrugged. "If anybody doubted my ability, they couldn't say so. I was born to my position."

"You proved you could do a good job, though."

"It isn't always mentioned in the articles about me," he drawled. "They prefer to dwell on my social life."

Suzanna had seen pictures of him on yachts and in the latest clubs, always accompanied by a group of the beautiful people. So she knew all the talk about him wasn't just hype. It didn't seem politic to mention it now, however.

"Would you have chosen to be king if you'd had a choice?" she asked instead.

"I've never really thought about it," he answered slowly. "My destiny was preordained from the day I was born. The House of Souverain dates back hundreds of years. Our motto is Serve With Honor."

"That's a pretty weighty burden for a child to have hanging over him," Suzanna observed.

"It didn't intimidate me. I was a holy terror as a kid, unlike my brother, Kenneth, who never got into trouble. On the few occasions when he did something wrong, I got blamed for it." Morgan laughed. "Nobody could believe little Kenny would misbehave."

"That must not have endeared him to you."

"I might have been annoyed at the time, but it didn't affect our relationship. We've always been close, and even more so since our parents died."

Suzanna had read up a little on Monrovia before she left home. She knew that Morgan's parents had died within a few months of each other from a rare virus contracted on a visit to a foreign country. That had been three years ago. Morgan was the youngest crowned head in Europe, when he ascended the throne at only thirty-two.

"Your brother isn't married either, is he?"

"No, the Souverain men are slow bloomers."

They must have a different definition of the term, Suzanna thought. How much more polished and experienced could he get?

His laughing expression turned serious. "Marriage is taken lightly in some parts of the world today, but not in Monrovia. When I marry it will be forever."

"You mean, royalty has its privileges, but also its obligations."

"I don't consider it a hardship. The girl I marry will be the woman I couldn't imagine living without."

Suzanna couldn't help envying the lucky girl who became his queen. A ripple of excitement shivered up her spine as she thought about what it would be like to be married to this charismatic man!

"No comment? You don't believe in living happily ever after?"

"Yes… yes, I do," she answered breathlessly.

"Is there a young man at home waiting impatiently for your return?"

"No, I'm not involved with anyone."

"There must be many men who would welcome the opportunity." He gave her an admiring glance. "But you're wise to wait for the right man to come along."

"Not according to my parents. They'd like me to get married and present them with grandchildren."

"My parents felt the same way." Morgan's smile

was tinged with sadness. "Kenneth and I were both a disappointment to them in that respect. Otherwise, we were a very close family."

"Ours is, too. I think my parents are great, and they tell everybody I'm the perfect daughter. Of course they have nothing to compare me to." Suzanna grinned. "I'm an only child."

"I suppose that has its advantages. You didn't have to share your toys."

"I'd rather have had a brother or sister."

He nodded. "There has always been a strong bond between Kenneth and me, in spite of the fact that we're completely different."

"I've never seen a picture of him," Suzanna remarked. "Or read much about him, either."

Morgan chuckled. "I told you we were different."

"How much younger than you is he?"

"Four years. Kenneth is…" He paused as the door flew open.

A young man burst into the room unceremoniously. He had a shock of blonde hair and laughing brown eyes. Suzanna had gotten friendly with Brian Dunphee because they were among the handful of Americans imported to work at the castle.

He was a master craftsman, skilled at the decorative scrollwork formerly used on walls and ceilings of ancient churches and castles. It was an almost extinct art form that he'd learned from his grandfather.

"Hey, Suzie," he called. "I just heard the big enchilada is making an inspection. Just thought I'd warn—" He stopped abruptly on seeing Morgan.

"Oh! Sorry, Your Highness. I didn't know you... I mean, I didn't mean to interrupt anything."

The king stood in one lithe movement, looking very regal in spite of his casual attire. His face was expressionless as he gazed at the young man. "Do you work here?" he asked.

"Well, yeah, I... uh... I'm part of the renovation crew repairing the east tower."

"How is the work progressing?"

"Just great! It's beginning to look real good."

"I'll have to drop by and see it." Morgan glanced at his wristwatch. "But not today. I seem to have run out of time. You can tell your crew the big enchilada won't be coming by." With an amused look, the king went out the door.

"Jeez!" The young man smacked his forehead with the heel of his hand. "I really stepped in it that time, didn't I? Who knew the king would be hanging out in your studio like a normal person? What was he doing here, anyway?"

"He came to see how the restoration is going," Suzanna said.

Brian raised one sandy-colored eyebrow. "He seemed kind of ticked off at being interrupted. Are you sure you don't have a little something going with His Highness?"

"Yeah, right! The poor guy can't get a date, so he has to hit on the hired help."

"You're not too bad looking. I'll bet you'd clean up real good." He gave her paint-stained outfit a laughing glance.

"If that's your idea of a compliment, you could take lessons from the king."

"Aha! I knew there was something going on between you two! I could feel it the minute I came in the room. I'm an authority on sexual tension."

"Don't be ridiculous. I just meant he's very polished and sophisticated. We were discussing art when you burst in like gangbusters. The king is understandably concerned about his paintings. His collection is priceless."

"Art isn't the only thing he collects. He's also partial to beautiful women."

"Don't try to butter me up," Suzanna joked. "You just implied that I'm a mess."

"You know better. I'm merely offering a word of warning. It might be a hoot to sleep with a king—just don't expect more than a pleasant memory."

Pleasant? That was a pretty pallid word to describe a night of love with King Morgan. The man had the body of an Adonis and a face to match! But Brian was right, he was out of her league.

"Thanks for the advice," she said crisply. "But I'm not the groupie type. I didn't come here looking for romance, I came to do a job."

"People have been known to combine the two," he observed.

"It's not a good idea, even if the boss isn't a king. All I intend to take home from Monrovia is a big, fat paycheck."

"I will say the guy is generous. Of course, he has enough money to buy a small continent. No wonder women throw themselves at him."

"You've got to be kidding!"

"Okay, I'll admit he's a hunk." Brian laughed. "All the more reason to play it safe around him. Well, I'd better get back on the job."

After he left, Suzanna didn't return to work immediately. Her encounter with the king had made a disturbing impact. Admittedly he was something special, but she was no starry-eyed teenager. Several handsome, successful men had been in love with her, and she hadn't gotten all soft and breathless. When King Morgan looked at her with that amber glow in his eyes, she melted like an ice-cream cone in a microwave. Even though she knew that charm of his was automatic.

She was making entirely too much out of their brief meeting, Suzanna finally decided. Her response to him was understandable. After all, how many people got a chance to chat with a king, one on one? It was natural to be excited, a normal reaction to a once-in-a-lifetime experience.

She pulled her stool closer to the worktable. These surroundings were responsible for her inexplicably girlish behavior. Living in an ancient castle in a romantic little country was like living in a dream world. King Morgan was part of a fairy tale that would end when the job did. They would both live happily ever after—only in different countries.

Chapter Two

Morgan's unexpectedly lengthy visit with Suzanna threw his schedule off. There were always people waiting to see him with various matters that needed his decision. Most of them were problems they could have solved themselves if they'd just used common sense, he thought impatiently. He should be able to take an hour off for personal reasons without panicking everybody.

Not that his visit with Suzanna was personal, he told himself as he walked back to the far wing of the castle. He'd gone to get a firsthand report on the restoration. Morgan smiled wryly at himself, not being into self-deception. A personal inspection had been his original intention. He'd stayed because Suzanna Bentley was an intriguing woman, a combination of brains and beauty.

She had the face of an angel and a wickedly alluring body. What a combination!

Morgan didn't have time to dwell on Suzanna after he returned to his office. As expected, his secretary was waiting with a full agenda, every item of which the man considered vital.

"I have a list of urgent telephone calls that need to be returned, Your Highness. And the finance minister will be here for his appointment momentarily." The man's disapproving tone of voice hinted that the king's presence was long overdue, although he couldn't come right out and say so. "There are also a number of people who wish me to set up an audience with Your Highness."

"There always are. Put the list on my desk."

"It's already there, sire."

A young man joined them as Morgan picked up the sheet of paper. The king's frown of concentration disappeared when he glanced up and saw his brother.

Other than a slight family resemblance to the king, Kenneth de Souverain was completely different in appearance. His hair was fair rather than dark like Morgan's, and he had a much slighter build. He did have the same regal carriage, but not the strong jaw or commanding manner.

"Where did you disappear to?" Kenneth asked. "I've been calling you for an hour."

"Don't tell me I had an appointment with you, too?"

"No, I just wanted to go over a couple of things with you. Did you skip out on your royal duties?"

"Not really. I went to check on how the repair

work is progressing in the east wing. It took longer than I expected.''

''Could you tell if the crew is doing a good job, or did you just nod your head and look wise?''

''It works every time.'' Morgan laughed. ''What did you want to see me about?''

''I need to go over a couple of details for the party tonight.''

Morgan's smile faded. ''I'm still not comfortable about this party. It doesn't seem right, since the country is still in mourning for the Queen Mother. I called for a year's moratorium on all state festivities.''

''This is a private birthday party, not a state occasion. You canceled the usual hoopla—the fireworks and barbecues and so forth. But even a king gets to celebrate his birthday. There will only be thirty or forty people, just relatives and close friends.''

''Well, it's too late to call it off now.''

''Grandmother wouldn't have wanted you to,'' Kenneth said. ''Remember how she loved parties? She had a tea for a group of her friends just a week before she got sick.''

Morgan sighed. ''It's hard to believe Grandmother has been gone for six months. She was so indomitable.''

''The entire country misses her, but we have to remember that she had a long, happy life.''

''She neither looked nor acted ninety-three,'' Morgan said fondly.

''That's certainly true.'' Kenneth hesitated before changing the subject. ''About tonight. I hope you don't mind, but I invited Alicia Marquette to the party. I really had no choice. We ran into each other at the yacht club. Somebody there mentioned your birthday and one thing led to another. I felt obligated to—''

''There's no need for a long explanation,'' Morgan interrupted. ''She's perfectly welcome.''

''Well, I know Sophia is coming.''

''So are a number of other charming young ladies.''

''I don't know how you juggle all these relationships, Morgan,'' his brother said with a mixture of admiration and impatience.

''You sound like the *National Informer*,'' Morgan said disgustedly. ''If I had as many affairs as they accuse me of, I wouldn't have time to run the country!''

''Those articles are irresponsible and unfair! You've carried on Father's work brilliantly. Monrovia couldn't have a harder working king.''

Morgan's scowl relaxed in a grin. ''Are you telling me this because it's my birthday?''

''No, it's the truth. I'm just glad I didn't create problems by inviting Alicia. Sophia doesn't welcome competition. She's quite possessive, and Alicia can't hide her attraction to you.''

''I'm the object of her fantasies this month,'' Morgan said dismissively. ''Next month it will be somebody else. She's still very young. As for Sophia, we're just friends. There's been no commitment on either side.''

''You must know she'd like one.''

''Countess Sophia Duvain, along with a lot of other

lovely ladies, would like to be queen of Monrovia,'' Morgan said dryly. ''I'm under no illusions about that.''

Before Kenneth could answer, the secretary appeared in the doorway. ''Excuse me for interrupting, Your Highness, but the finance minister is here for his appointment.''

Most of the castle repair crew were native Monrovians who worked regular shifts and went home in the evening. The foreign workers like Suzanna and Brian were provided not only with rooms, but with dining and recreational facilities, as well. They were given security badges that enabled them to come and go on their own time, but it was easier to eat most of their meals in the dining hall, especially during the week. Transportation into the nearby city was a hassle.

That night after dinner Suzanna watched a movie on television in the lounge with Brian and two artisans from Italy who were skilled in masonry work. They'd been employed to repair the gargoyles decorating the outside of the east wing tower. Since their work and Brian's involved physical labor, the men were yawning before the film was over.

Suzanna wasn't tired, but she didn't feel like watching more television or reading a book. She felt restless and decided to take a walk around the grounds. It was a beautiful spring night, after a day that had been unusually warm for this time of year, native Monrovians said. It would be nice to get some fresh air after being cooped up in her studio all day.

The grounds were beautiful under a full moon that made everything look familiar yet indistinct, like a surrealist painting done in shades of black and gray. The gravel that paved the path glittered like moonstones and crunched under her feet.

On a whim, Suzanna took off her sandals and walked on the grass. It felt thick and spongy underfoot. The slight breeze felt good, too, on her bare arms and legs. She'd changed after work into a short cotton dress.

The parklike grounds made Suzanna feel as if she were in an enchanted forest inhabited by fairies and elves. Laughing at her own vivid imagination, she continued her stroll.

Suzanna didn't notice that she had walked the considerable length of the castle, all the way to the west wing that housed the royal apartments and various reception rooms. Lights were streaming out of tall French windows that opened onto a terrace, and a babble of voices drifted out into the night.

As she drew closer Suzanna could see that a party was taking place in a large drawing room. Satin draperies were looped back from the windows, giving her a clear view of the exquisite furnishings. A crowd of elegantly dressed men and women were milling about, laughing and talking, while servants circulated among them refilling champagne glasses and passing hors d'oeuvres.

Suzanna didn't have to look for the king; he dominated the room. He'd been casually dressed earlier, and she thought he was striking looking then. But tonight, in a white dinner jacket and black trousers, he was drop-dead gorgeous!

His unruly dark hair was tamed, and the white jacket accentuated his tanned face. As he inclined his head, listening with a smile to the beautiful redhead beside him, King Morgan was the epitome of sophistication.

The redhead was no slouch, either. She had on a skintight, low-cut evening gown that showed off her excellent figure as well as a lot of bosom. Around her neck was a glittering necklace that looked fabulous. Could those be real rubies? Suzanna moved closer for a better look.

The peaceful night was unexpectedly shattered by someone shouting and the frenzied sound of dogs barking nearby. Suddenly it occurred to Suzanna that she could be mistaken for a Peeping Tom. The romantic scene taking place in the graceful drawing room was like watching a movie, but someone else might have a different interpretation. Instinctively she started to hurry off into the shadows.

A commanding voice shouted, "Stop right there!"

Suzanna panicked when she realized the dogs were closing in on her. Her only thought was to reach the nearest tree and try to climb to safety. She didn't make it. The nightmare accelerated when she was knocked to the ground by a large black dog that stood over her, snarling. He was joined by the rest of the pack, which eddied around her with menacing, bared teeth.

"Don't move or they'll tear you to pieces," the warning voice said. Several guards had caught up with the dogs. "Who are you and what are you doing here?" one of them asked.

"I work here," she said in a voice that was barely above a whisper.

"Speak up! If you work here, where's your badge?"

Suzanna started to sit up, then quickly changed her mind when the lead dog growled deep in his throat and the rest set up a renewed clamor. "I don't have it with me, but I really do work in the castle. I was just taking a walk."

"You'll have to do better than that. Why were you spying on the king?"

Before she could explain that she wasn't spying, the French doors of the drawing room opened and people spilled out onto the patio.

"What the devil is going on out here?" Morgan demanded.

"We caught a prowler, but there's no need for concern, Your Highness. We'll deal with her."

"Her?" Morgan walked onto the lawn for a better look. "Good Lord, man, call off the dogs!" he ordered when he saw them clustered around Suzanna's prone body.

She sat up gratefully.

Morgan peered at her in the dim light. "Suzanna? What are you doing here?"

"We caught her looking in that window over there, Your Highness," the guard said.

She was glad the darkness covered her hot cheeks. "It wasn't like that at all! He totally misunderstood."

"Then why did you run when I told you to stop?" the guard demanded.

"I was trying to get away from those vicious dogs." She eyed them warily. "Can I get up now?"

"Of course." Morgan put out a hand to help her to her feet. "I'll take over from here," he told the guard. "You can go back to your posts."

Suzanna was still trembling after the traumatic occurrence. Her legs buckled when she tried to stand.

"Steady." Morgan put an arm around her waist. "I'm sure it was a frightening experience, but you're safe now," he said in a soothing voice. "The dogs didn't hurt you, did they?"

"No, I'm just embarrassed about the whole thing. I wasn't spying on you," she said carefully. "The guard wouldn't give me a chance to explain."

"What were you doing out here in the dark?" Morgan looked at her curiously.

"I was simply taking a walk." She moved out of his embrace, but her legs were still wobbly.

He reached out and lifted her into his arms. "You need to lie down for a while."

"I'm fine. It's just a normal reaction to being chased by killer dogs," she said, trying to make a joke out of the incident. "I'll be okay except for recurring nightmares."

When he turned toward the drawing room, they both realized that most of the party were still assembled on the patio, watching them with interest.

"What happened, Morgan?" someone called.

"Is anything wrong?"

A chorus of voices pelted him with questions.

"Everything is under control. You can all go back to the party," Morgan said with authority.

The guests complied, some of them, like the red-head, reluctantly. She kept glancing over her shoulder as Morgan carried Suzanna through another door into a luxurious den.

After placing her on a down-filled sofa he went to a bar in one of the paneled walls and poured amber liquid from a cut-glass decanter into a crystal glass. Suzanna started to sit up when he returned and handed her the glass, but he gently urged her back against the pillows.

Seating himself on the edge of the couch facing her, he said, "Drink this. It will calm you down."

"I'm fine now," she protested, but she did as he said. The fiery liquid made her eyes water. Blinking her long eyelashes, she said, "What did you give me? You don't happen to be related to the Borgias, do you?"

Morgan laughed. "That was hundred-year-old-brandy."

"Well, that explains it! It's gone bad," she joked.

"I can see your education has been sorely ne-glected," he said with amusement. "Fine brandy is one of life's little pleasures, along with fine wine."

"The only thing I know about wine is that some are red and some are white."

"Shocking! I look forward to furthering your ed-ucation."

The mood between them had changed subtly. Su-zanna was abruptly aware of the intimacy of the sit-uation. She felt vulnerable lying on the couch with

Morgan smiling down at her, their hips touching as they shared a cushion meant for one.

She stirred tentatively, hoping he'd take the hint and let her up. "I'm keeping you from your party. Your guests must be wondering what happened to you."

"Yes, I suppose so." He continued to gaze at her. "Are you sure you feel well enough to walk all the way back to the east wing?"

"No problem. After that brandy I might just fly back." She smiled weakly, raising herself up on her elbows, since she couldn't sit up. That would put her in his arms—again!

"All right, if you're sure." He rose, finally. "Maybe you'd better return through the castle to avoid any more mishaps on the grounds."

Suzanna scrambled off the couch hurriedly. "That's a good idea. I'll do that."

He noticed for the first time that she was barefoot. "What happened to your shoes?"

She groaned. "I took them off while I was walking. They're out there someplace."

Morgan pulled a velvet cord on the wall. "I'll send a servant out to get them."

"Please don't bother," she begged. Her embarrassment was mounting by the minute. Was there anything else she could do to look stupid? "They're just a pair of old sandals. I'll look for them tomorrow."

"Nonsense. It's a long way to the east wing. You might step on something and hurt yourself." He turned to the servant who had answered his summons almost instantly, and gave the man instructions on where to look for the missing shoes.

"You don't have to stay here with me," Suzanna said after the servant left.

"I'm aware of that, but while we're waiting you can tell me why you were taking a solitary walk around the grounds. Don't you have anything better to do at night?"

"The castle is rather isolated. Those of us who live here don't have transportation to go anywhere. We wouldn't know where to go anyway, since we're strangers to Monrovia."

Morgan frowned. "I didn't know your options were so limited."

"Not at all. You've been most generous. We have television and a well-stocked library. The men are usually tired at night anyway, since they do physical labor. I simply felt like taking a walk tonight because it was so lovely out."

While they were talking, the servant returned carrying the pair of shoes. "That was quick," Morgan commented.

"They were right where you said they might be, Your Highness." The man bowed and left the room.

In her hurry to put on her shoes and leave, Suzanna tried to step into them and almost tripped.

Morgan urged her gently onto a chair and hunkered down in front of her.

When he took her foot in his hand, she looked at him in amazement. "What are you doing?"

"I'm helping you on with your shoes before you fall again."

"I can do that. I'm not completely incompetent," she mumbled, trying to pull her foot away.

His hand closed around her ankle and he placed her foot on his knee while he reached for her shoe. The situation was unreal and too sensuous for comfort. Her mouth felt dry as she imagined his hand sliding up her leg.

Morgan had no such intentions. He looked at her with laughing eyes as he slid her right foot into the sandal. "Indulge me. I'm fulfilling a fantasy." As her pulse rate speeded up he added, "I've always wondered if I could make it in some other profession. Like a shoe salesman, for instance. Am I doing it right?"

"You remind me more of Prince Charming trying the glass slipper on all the ladies in the kingdom," she said lightly. "But I guess you wouldn't care to be demoted to a prince."

"You'd make a lovely Cinderella," he said in a deep velvet voice, gazing into her eyes.

Suzanna was transfixed by the golden glow, even though common sense told her this was an act he could turn on and off at will. Damn, but he was good at it, though! She felt the warmth from his hand spreading throughout her entire body.

She was gazing at him with unconsciously parted lips when the door opened and the redhead flounced in.

"What's keeping you, Morgan? Everybody is—" She stopped abruptly with a sharp intake of breath.

He handed Suzanna her left shoe and stood unhurriedly. "Miss Bentley was badly shaken up. I was making sure she felt well enough to return to her room.''

"What room? Who *is* she?'' The redhead's hostile stare swept over Suzanna, taking note of her ruffled hair and flushed cheeks.

"Miss Suzanna Bentley, Countess Sophia Duvain.'' Morgan made the introductions.

After the two women had acknowledged each other tepidly, Suzanna moved quickly to the door saying, "Well, I'll let you get back to your party.''

Almost before the door closed, Sophia repeated her earlier question. "Who is that woman? And why is she staying here in the castle?''

A flicker of annoyance crossed Morgan's face, but it wasn't evident in his voice. "Why do you ask? Did you think you'd met her before?''

"Good heavens, no! Where would our paths ever cross?''

"They did tonight,'' he pointed out.

"All right, Morgan, don't tell me,'' she said petulantly.

"There's no reason not to. Miss Bentley is a very talented art restorer. She came from America to salvage the paintings that were damaged in the fire.''

Sophia's face cleared. "She's one of the workmen!''

"I doubt if she could pass for a man,'' he drawled. "But I suppose workwoman would sound awkward, even in these politically correct times.''

There was a light tap at the door before the king's brother entered. "Is everything all right, Morgan?''

"Yes, we were just about to rejoin the party." He stood aside for Sophia to precede him.

The redhead stuck closely to his side from then on, trailing after Morgan as he moved from group to group. She put her hand on his arm when they were joined by a pretty young blonde in her mid-twenties.

Morgan appeared to listen to everybody, but he didn't take part in the conversations. His thoughts were on Suzanna and the way she had felt in his arms tonight. The thin cotton dress had made it apparent, when he cradled her body against his chest, that she wasn't wearing much underneath the dress. Not that she needed anything. Her breasts were naturally high and firm, and her body was taut, yet yielding, in his arms.

If he had the talent, he'd like to paint her nude. She would be magnificent posed on a couch with her sapphire eyes veiled by those incredible black lashes, and her lips softly parted. What a painting that would make!

Except that he would never get around to picking up a brush. If ever a woman was made for love, this one was. Morgan smiled at his own erotic fancies. Considering that he barely knew the girl, his intimate knowledge of her body was only a fortuitous accident—at least, it was a happy event for *him*.

At the midnight supper that was served, many toasts were offered. Some of the them were in memory of the Queen Mother, but most were humorous tributes to the king on his birthday.

When the guests finally left, Morgan and Kenneth

went into the den for a final nightcap to unwind before going to bed.

"Aren't you glad now that I talked you into having a party?" Kenneth asked.

"Yes, I'll have to admit it was very entertaining," Morgan answered. "I think everyone enjoyed it more than the usual mammoth celebrations."

"Sophia liked it better." Kenneth grinned.

"You think so? She's very partial to grand balls."

"But she got to spend more time with you tonight. That's Sophia's goal in life. She was very irritated when you were so charming to Alicia." Kenneth slanted a glance at his brother. "You might choose to dismiss it as a schoolgirl crush, but Alicia is definitely attracted to you."

"I'm very flattered, but I assure you it's just a passing fancy. She'll find someone more suitable."

"Alicia is very suitable," Kenneth said evenly. "She's young and beautiful, she has an impeccable reputation and she's a princess in her own right. What more could you ask?"

"Rank isn't the first thing I look for in a woman," Morgan answered dryly.

"What *are* you looking for? We're brothers, and I don't know any more than anyone else does."

"I don't think most people go shopping with a list of specifications. I want what any other man wants, a girl who loves me for what I am, not who I am, somebody I can talk to and laugh with." Without conscious thought, Suzanna flashed into Morgan's mind, the way she'd looked tonight—slightly disheveled, which made her adorably provocative.

"That's certainly reasonable," Kenneth said. "And it isn't beyond the realm of possibility. Haven't you ever met anyone who fit the profile?"

Morgan laughed. "Well, maybe I left out one thing. There has to be that little spark of magic between us."

"I know what you mean," Kenneth said softly.

Morgan looked at him with interest. "Is there something you're not telling me?"

"I don't know what you mean."

"Now I'm sure you're holding out on me. Who is she and why haven't you let me meet her?"

"You're too much competition," Kenneth answered with a weak smile.

"Surely you can't think I'd try to cut you out!" Morgan said indignantly.

"You're not the problem, big brother," Kenneth said, still trying to sound joking. "What if she's the one who decides she's in love with *you?*"

"You take her to have her head examined. Bring her over and I'll tell her she got the prize brother."

"I don't know about that, but I'll consider it." Kenneth stood and stretched. "Well, I think I'll turn in."

Morgan stopped him with a concerned look on his handsome face. "I hope you know I'm always here for you, Ken—if you want to talk about anything, or for any other reason."

"Don't you have enough to do running the country?" Kenneth smiled.

"I'll never be too busy for *you.*"

"I know that, and you can stop worrying. My only

problem right now is how I'm going to get up in the morning and look reasonably intelligent at that seminar on trade relations I'm supposed to preside over.''

Morgan grinned. ''Just keep saying you'll take the matter under advisement and get back to them.''

Suzanna was in her studio early the next morning, as usual. But that day she didn't seem to be accomplishing much. Perhaps because she kept wondering if King Morgan was going to put in an appearance.

You're being ridiculous, Suzanna told herself. Why would he? He'd no doubt seen more than enough of her yesterday! She was still embarrassed at the memory of how she'd disrupted his party. He hadn't seemed annoyed, though. In fact, he'd been quite solicitous. The king was actually a very nice man.

It was almost lunchtime when Morgan finally showed up at the studio. By then, Suzanna no longer expected him and was engrossed in her work. His footsteps on the bare floor alerted her, and she glanced up, thinking it was Brian or one of the other workmen.

''I came to see how you were feeling this morning after your little mishap,'' he said.

''No ill effects. How was your party?'' she asked, trying to appear relaxed. How did one make small talk with a king? She never had this problem with ordinary men. But King Morgan was far from ordinary!

''Very pleasant. People have to be nice to you on your birthday.'' He smiled.

''I didn't know it was your birthday!''

"There's no reason why you should. In view of my advanced age, we skipped the balloons and paper hats."

"I can't imagine the redhea—the countess in a paper hat."

"She'd be even more shocked at the idea." He laughed.

"Did you at least have a birthday cake?" Suzanna asked hurriedly.

"A gigantic one, but with only a symbolic candle on it. I suppose they didn't want to risk starting another fire."

"You're not old enough to fish for compliments," she joked.

"Sometimes it works," he said with amusement. "You never know until you try."

"I should think in your position you'd get more than your share of flattery."

"The danger there is if you start believing it," the king said dryly. He glanced at his watch. "I only have a few minutes before my next appointment. I just stopped by to see if you were all right."

"That was very thoughtful, but I told you I'm okay. Fortunately I only hit my head—the thickest part of me." She laughed.

"You didn't tell me you were injured," he said with a frown.

"I wasn't! It's just a little bump. You can hardly feel it."

"You should have told me last night. I would have had my physician check you out." He moved in back of her and lifted her long hair.

"You can't see anything." She tried to twitch away, but his hands cupped her chin and tilted her head back so she was looking up at him.

"Show me where it is," he ordered.

She gave up and touched a spot a couple of inches below her crown.

His long fingers replaced hers and gently probed the small bump. "Does it hurt when I do this?" he asked.

"No," she murmured, feeling her whole body relax. His fingers were making circles around the area, looking for other bumps, and the slow massage felt incredibly sensuous. She closed her eyes and tried not to purr.

Morgan looked down at the dark lashes fanning her cheeks. They were extraordinarily long, but he had a feeling they weren't false, like the ones many women wore. Suzanna didn't need any artificial help; she was blessed by nature. Unconsciously his hands slid down to the nape of her neck and stroked the soft skin.

"Mmm, that feels wonderful," she remarked dreamily. "You'd make an even better masseur than you would a shoe salesman."

"Those are only two of my talents. I have more," he said in a silky voice.

That brought her abruptly to her senses. She slid quickly out of her chair and stood facing him.

"Was it something I said?" His eyes danced mischievously.

"People wander in and out of here all the time," she said coolly, hiding her discomfort. "I wouldn't want them to get the wrong idea."

"You're probably right. My intentions were completely honorable, but I don't want to compromise you in any way." There was still a trace of amusement on his face, but it wasn't evident in his tone. "One other thing before I go," he added. "You'll be getting a bulletin about it. I've arranged for a car and driver to be available to take you and the crew anywhere you'd like to go after hours and on the weekend."

"That's very generous of you."

He shrugged. "There's no reason for all of you to be stuck here during your free time. Everybody needs some recreation and a change of scenery. I'm just glad you brought the matter to my attention. I also instructed my secretary to include a list of local attractions some of you might want to visit."

"You're certainly a thoughtful employer, Your Highness."

"Don't you think it's time we were on a first-name basis? Why don't you call me Morgan?"

"I don't think I should do that," she said uncertainly.

"Why not?"

"Well... it doesn't seem respectful. You are the king."

"But you're not one of my subjects."

"That's true, but I'm living in your country. I should abide by your rules."

"I don't know if it's an actual rule that my subjects have to address me in a certain way. That's an interesting point. We'll have to discuss it, but I don't have the time right now. Come to my apartment for a drink after you finish work.''

The invitation was so unexpected that Suzanna could only stare at him as he headed for the door, taking her silence as acceptance. By the time she pulled herself together, the king had disappeared.

Don't you know how to say no? she asked herself disgustedly.

It was a terrible idea to go to the king's apartment for any reason! The invitation had been delivered casually—almost as an afterthought—but Suzanna wasn't fooled for a moment. King Morgan was a highly sophisticated man who knew how to get what he wanted. And all indications pointed to her as his fancy of the week.

She wasn't worried that he'd be insistent. A man like Morgan could get all the willing women he wanted. But if he became a little too friendly and she discouraged him, the situation could turn sticky. It had been Suzanna's experience that men had fragile egos. What if he found some rationalization for sending her home? She was really enjoying her work, and the pay was fantastic.

On the other hand, King Morgan had a richly satisfying life of his own. He didn't need to lie awake nights figuring out ways to seduce one of his employees.

She'd been presented with a rare opportunity to see how royalty actually lived, the private apartment where the ruler of a country took off his jacket and read the evening newspaper. Wouldn't she be crazy not to simply relax and enjoy herself, instead of looking for reasons not to?

The answer was so obvious that Suzanna began to think about what to wear.

Chapter Three

Suzanna's eyes were bright with anticipation when she knocked on one of the carved double doors to the king's apartment that night. After only an instant, it was opened by a liveried servant.

"Miss Bentley to see King Morgan," she said briskly, to set the right tone.

Without a word, the man motioned for her to follow him. A hallway led from the foyer, which was as large as a room in a normal house. Suzanna had time for only a glimpse of several jade boxes on a marble-topped console table, and an intriguing watercolor on one wall, softly lit by the crystal chandelier overhead.

The hall led past a large, sumptuously furnished living room and a dining room of comparable size. This really was an apartment, not just a suite. The servant led her to a cozier den—if anything in this stately castle could be called cozy. The fireplace was immense, but it was flanked by comfortable couches and a big square table strewn with books and magazines. Then Morgan stood and dominated the room.

"I was beginning to think you weren't coming," he said.

"How could I pass up a chance to see how royalty lives?" Suzanna said lightly. "This apartment is spectacular!"

"I would have preferred to be the attraction, but I'm glad you're here." He smiled.

"You're always the main attraction, Your Highness," she said demurely.

"How can I convince you to call me Morgan?"

"That would take some getting used to," she said tentatively.

"It shouldn't be so hard," he coaxed. "You Americans are pretty laid-back people."

"That's true. At home, everybody calls you by your first name, from the gas station attendant to your doctor."

"Well, there you are." He evidently considered the matter settled. "What can I get you to drink?"

She glanced at the tall glass on the table next to where he'd been sitting. "I'll have whatever you're having."

"Actually that's iced tea, but I can fix you whatever you like."

"Iced tea would be nice."

When he walked over to a bar cart that held an

assortment of bottles, mixes and a silver ice bucket, she was surprised. "You're going to get it yourself?"

He gave her a puzzled look. When her meaning became clear, his mouth curved ironically. "It wasn't too hard to learn how to pour from a pitcher. I also tie my own shoes."

"There are so many servants around here that it wouldn't surprise me if tying shoes was a job classification. You're like the man who didn't play tennis because he could afford to pay somebody to do it for him."

"You have an outdated view of royalty," Morgan said with amusement. "The days are gone when monarchs grew fat and lazy because every whim was gratified without any effort on their part. That's history. In these modern times, rulers are more comparable to executives of a large company."

"Not exactly. You can't be fired."

"I can be deposed. It's more trouble and takes longer than a pink slip on your desk, but it can be done."

"Wouldn't you have to do something really horrendous?" she asked.

"It would be unusual for the monarch of an established country with a long lineage to be forced off the throne, but it's theoretically possible. There are always castle intrigues." He shrugged. "That hasn't changed."

"I think I'd find it uncomfortable to be surrounded by people who might be plotting against me," she said slowly.

"If you have the love and respect of your subjects,

you have nothing to worry about.'' His eyes suddenly began to dance mischievously. "Too bad you're not one of my subjects.''

"I respect you,'' she said demurely.

"I suppose one out of two isn't bad.'' His hand brushed hers and Suzanna's nerves went on red alert.

But Morgan was merely reaching for her glass. "Let me put some more ice in that. Are you sure you wouldn't like anything stronger?''

"No, the tea is very refreshing. I really shouldn't drink on an empty stomach, anyway. I skipped lunch today because I got so interested in the Vermeer I was restoring that I forgot all about eating.'' Suzanna knew she was babbling, but the king had that effect on her.

He returned and handed her the refilled glass, then sat next to her. She couldn't help tensing as he stretched his arm casually along the back of the couch. He looked so handsome and virile—and completely relaxed. Not like a man who was about to make a pass, she scolded herself. But why had he invited her here tonight? Why did he ask her to call him by his first name?

Morgan was watching her enigmatically. "You once asked me if I liked being king. The answer is yes, except for occasions like this.''

Suzanna gave him a puzzled look. "I don't understand.''

"If I were an ordinary man you wouldn't be wondering if I was going to kiss you.''

Her cheeks bloomed with color, but she couldn't help laughing. "Yes, I would.''

"Maybe that was a bad example. You're a beautiful woman, and many men must have wanted to make love to you. But let me put it another way—under normal circumstances, if I tried to kiss you, either you'd respond or you'd tell me I was out of line. Either way, it wouldn't be a big deal—if I wasn't a king."

"Okay, that's true." She sighed. "I'll admit I've been nervous around you, but it's understandable."

"Not to me. Perhaps you'll be good enough to enlighten me."

"You've been linked to some of the most glamorous women in the world. Why would you be interested in me?" she asked bluntly. "The most obvious reason explains why I've been so wary."

"Your opinion of me is not very favorable, but you should think more highly of yourself."

"I'm not being coy or fishing for compliments. I've had my share of male attention, but I'm a realist. I know I can't compare to the women you run around with. It's difficult, however, to tell a king—who also happens to be your employer—that you don't want to play those games. Naturally I've been a little edgy."

"I don't play those games, either. Even the tabloids haven't suggested I made love to an unwilling woman."

"I wasn't afraid you'd use force," Suzanna said carefully.

"Only that my male pride would be so wounded by your refusal to sleep with me that I'd fire you." His expression was a mixture of amusement and irritation. "Don't you think I've ever been turned down before?"

"Not often," she replied truthfully.

"I'd like to think you believe my success rate is due to my charm, not my position. No, don't answer that. Maybe it's better that I don't know." He smiled. "I'd prefer to clear up the misunderstanding between us. I'm not a lecherous man with a secret agenda. I asked you here tonight because I enjoy talking to you."

"I feel pretty silly," she said wryly. "I just set a record for jumping to conclusions."

"We just had a slight misunderstanding, that's all. How long do you think the complete restoration will take?"

"Quite a while, I'm afraid. I've barely started and it's very painstaking work."

"I'm in no hurry. I want it done right, not fast." He slanted a glance at her. "But how about you? Will it be a hardship for you to be away from home for that long? You said you come from a very close family."

"Close in spirit. My parents live in Philadelphia, but I moved to New York City several years ago. I keep in touch by phone and I go home often, especially for holidays."

"Yes, those are family times. All of our relatives and old friends used to gather here for big celebrations." His eyes were shadowed. "It isn't the same anymore."

It was sad that he'd lost most of the people closest to him. Suzanna tried to lighten his mood. "It must be nice to have a formal dining room with enough seating for everybody. I'll bet you didn't have to bring in the kitchen chairs and the step stool like we did at our house.''

''No, our celebrations were festive, but quite formal. I remember the first time our parents decided Kenneth and I were old enough to join the adults for a holiday dinner. We felt so grown up.'' Morgan's expression cleared as he recalled that long-ago event. ''We soon discovered it was a privilege we could have done without. The grown-ups talked about politics and other things we weren't interested in, and dinner seemed to go on interminably.''

''Those formal affairs are hard on children,'' Suzanna agreed. ''They get fidgety.''

''We weren't allowed to fidget. We were little princes.''

''You poor kids.'' She smiled sympathetically. ''It must have been torture.''

''We spread the pain around.'' Morgan grinned. ''I switched my grape juice for my dinner partner's wine while she wasn't looking. She was a very proper countess who was too well-bred to criticize her host's strange selection. Then while I got boisterously tipsy and threw my roll across the table at Kenneth, he choked on his meat. It came back up rather colorfully—all over a duchess's gown.''

''I'll bet you weren't invited back very soon, even if the hosts were your parents.''

As they laughed together, Suzanna felt her constraint slip away. She and Morgan talked about growing up and going to college. Their experiences were similar, even if their backgrounds weren't. Both were popular and involved in school activities. She was a cheerleader among other things, and he was student body president and captain of the soccer team.

"We've both been fortunate," Suzanna observed. "It's very trendy nowadays for people to blame somebody else for their less-than-perfect lives—parents who didn't love them, or an unrequited love affair. You and I don't have those complaints."

Morgan gazed at her with frank admiration. "I can't imagine anyone not returning your love."

She flushed with pleasure that she tried not to show. "You haven't done so badly yourself in the romance department."

"How do I know your experience isn't even greater than mine?" he teased. "Everything I do is publicized, but nobody is keeping track of *you.*"

"They'd lose interest fast," she said dismissively. "It would be like comparing vanilla ice cream to a hot fudge sundae."

"Assuming I'm the latter, I don't know if I like the analogy." His eyes twinkled mischievously. "A hot fudge sundae is cold underneath."

She didn't think any man as virile as Morgan could have that problem. He oozed sex appeal and had the male physique to back up the promise. If his girlfriends had any complaints, Suzanna was sure coldness wasn't one of them.

Before she could answer, the servant was back. "Prince Kenneth is here, Your Highness," he announced.

Suzanna wasn't visible from the door, so the prince

didn't see her at first. "You're not dressed, Morgan!" he exclaimed. "Why aren't you ready?"

The king was dressed casually in light gray slacks and a silk shirt with several buttons undone and the sleeves rolled up. When the prince came farther into the room, Suzanna saw that he was wearing elegantly tailored evening clothes.

Prince Kenneth had the cool, unapproachable air of an aristocrat. Unlike his brother, who was equally distinguished, people wouldn't be drawn to this man instantly. He was handsome in his own way, but he didn't have the king's vitality.

"Forgive me for barging in like this," Kenneth said, after noticing Suzanna. "I didn't know you had a guest."

As Morgan introduced them, she rose. "I didn't realize it was getting so late," she said to the king. "You should have told me I was keeping you from something."

"I was having much too good a time to care," he said gallantly.

"Thank you. I enjoyed it, too."

The prince was looking at her curiously. "Haven't we met before?"

She guessed that he vaguely remembered her from the embarrassing night of his brother's birthday party.

Morgan answered for her without referring to the incident. "Suzanna is a fine arts restorer. She very kindly came here to help us salvage the paintings that were damaged."

He made it sound as if she were doing them a favor. Which was very gracious of him, Suzanna thought, considering the whopping salary he was paying her.

Prince Kenneth became less reserved. "It's hard to believe anything survived the flames. You've no idea how traumatic the fire was."

"I can imagine," she answered. "It must have been awful, not knowing if everything would be burned beyond repair."

"Unfortunately we did lose part of the collection. The painting I regret most was a small Tiepolo. It was Mother's favorite, remember, Morgan?"

The king nodded. "We were just talking about Mother and Father. I was telling Suzanna about our childhood here in the castle—most memorably, our first formal dinner party."

Prince Kenneth's grin made him look more approachable. "Ten years later, the Duchess of Cordelle still wouldn't let me date her daughter." He glanced at his watch. "If we had more time, there are a lot of other stories you could tell."

Suzanna took the hint. "I'd love to hear them, but I have to leave."

Morgan walked her to the door. "I wish you didn't have to go, but I am due at a reception."

"I understand perfectly. Thanks again for the iced tea, and I hope you enjoy your evening."

After she left the royal wing and went back with the hired help, Suzanna felt like Cinderella. Not that her accommodations were spartan. Her room was comfortable, if not luxurious, and Morgan had certainly tried to make their living conditions enjoyable.

She suddenly realized that she'd started to think of

him as Morgan, not the king. After those first awkward few minutes together he'd seemed like just a
stimulating companion, a man she'd like to know better. That's how a lot of women got hooked, she told
herself derisively.

Suzanna had gotten used to the fact that Morgan
was unpredictable. He might turn up in her studio the
next day, or not for a week—or maybe his visits
would stop entirely. She was disappointed when she
didn't hear from him for several days, but not devastated. It was nice while it lasted, was the way she
looked at it.

Her detachment ended when the phone in the studio
rang about five o'clock one afternoon. Suzanna's days
were satisfying without Morgan, but his voice on the
other end of the line added that little extra zing.

"Are you almost through for the day?" he asked.

"No, I usually work quite a bit later," she answered. "Can I do anything for you?"

"Yes, I'd like to discuss something with you.
Could you come to my chambers?"

"Certainly! I'd be glad to." She couldn't keep the
enthusiasm out of her voice. "Just give me a few
minutes to change clothes."

"That won't be necessary. Just come as you are."

"I'm really quite a mess." Suzanna glanced down
ruefully at her casual outfit. She had on a pale blue
sweat suit that day, a bad choice for her kind of work.
There was a paint smear in front where her smock
had come open, and she'd gotten solvent on one of
her sleeves.

"I've seen you in your work clothes," Morgan said. "You don't have to change. Unfortunately I only have about an hour and I do want to talk to you."

"All right," she agreed reluctantly. If she insisted, he might wonder why it was so important to her to make a good appearance.

Suzanna sped through the hallways, speculating about what was on Morgan's mind that was so urgent.

She was so intent on her thoughts that she didn't notice the older man walking toward her in the corridor near the royal apartment.

"What are you doing here?" he demanded imperiously. "You don't belong in this part of the castle."

"I'm here to see the king," she said evenly, determined to rein in her temper.

"Oh, are you, now?" he sneered. "You just decided to stop by and pay His Majesty a visit?"

Suzanna gritted her teeth. "He asked me to come."

"Don't lie to me, girl! What are you really doing here?"

"I told—"

"No, I don't want to hear your lies," he interrupted. "Just get out immediately, and don't try to come back or I'll have you thrown in jail."

"If you would just check with the king," she began.

"I warned you. Guards!" He raised his voice and bellowed, "Guards! Get out here immediately!"

The formerly quiet hallway suddenly erupted with activity as uniformed guards swarmed out from hidden posts. To Suzanna's shocked eyes it looked like

an army. As they advanced on her, the king's door
flew open and Morgan appeared.

"What the devil is all that racket?" he demanded.

"I found this suspicious-looking woman near your
chambers, sire," the older man said. "I'm going to
have the guards search her and then lock her up."

"Are you out of your mind, Rudolph?" Morgan
exclaimed. "Does she look like a criminal?"

The man looked Suzanna over with disdain. "I can
tell she doesn't belong here. What was she doing
wandering alone in the royal wing? If she's part of
any conspiracy against you, we'll get it out of her."

"Miss Bentley is my guest!" Morgan said explo-
sively.

Rudolph frowned. "It would be a mistake to try to
shield the woman out of compassion, sire. A female
can be even deadlier than a male."

"Are you questioning my word?" Morgan asked
ominously.

"Certainly not, Your Highness. I'm merely concerned with the king's safety."

"Your concern is misplaced. I don't know how to
make myself any clearer. Miss Bentley is my invited
guest. I *want* her here. Do you understand? She happens to be part of our staff of restoration experts. You
will apologize to her immediately for your insulting
actions!" The king's voice was icy.

"I was doing my duty as I saw it, sire."

"Apologize," Morgan said implacably.

Rudolph flicked a glance at the soldiers. They were
standing as stiffly as robots, but he knew they were
drinking in every word. When the man turned back

to Suzanna, the enmity in his eyes was scorching. She was glad her job didn't depend on him. He wasn't a forgiving man and he would blame her for this humiliation.

"I'm sorry if I displeased you in any way," he told Suzanna in a toneless voice.

The unpleasant incident was over almost as suddenly as it started. Rudolph and the soldiers dispersed in different directions and Suzanna went into Morgan's apartment with him.

She tried to lighten the atmosphere, because his face was still stormy. "It might not be a bad idea to issue me a hallway pass, just in case you're not there to rescue me the next time I almost get thrown in jail."

"Rudolph Jablon is a jackass! I can only apologize for his unforgivable behavior."

"It's kind of exciting to be mistaken for a terrorist." Suzanna grinned. "My image has always been sort of bland."

"I'm glad you find it amusing. Rudolph is one of the ministers I inherited from my father's regime. He's a royal pain, but I suppose he's competent enough at his job. He's just such a joyless, one-dimensional man!" Morgan exclaimed in frustration. "The only thing he cares about is the monarchy."

"That's not such a bad thing," she said placatingly. "He's very loyal to you."

"I suppose, but he tries to manipulate me into doing things the way they've always been done. He doesn't realize that times change and new ideas aren't necessarily bad.'' Morgan's scowl showed his irritation.

''Your cabinet can't actually challenge your decisions, can they?'' Suzanna asked curiously. ''You're the king. I thought your word was absolute.''

''It is, but all the infighting makes my life difficult.'' Morgan's face cleared. ''I want to discuss something much more interesting. But first, let me fix you a drink. Did you skip lunch again today? I'll order some hors d'oeuvres.''

''That would be nice. Actually I did skip lunch.''

''Is that how you keep your lovely figure?'' His eyes swept over her with approval.

''How can you tell what it's like?'' She held her arms away from her sides. ''Most of the time I have on something shapeless, like this.''

''But not always.'' A little smile played around his firm mouth as he picked up a decanter. ''Besides, I have a good memory.''

Suzanna did, too. She remembered how scantily dressed she'd been the night Morgan had carried her from the garden.

The servant who answered the king's summons saved Suzanna from having to reply. After the man left, she made sure Morgan didn't return to the subject.

''What did you want to discuss with me?'' she asked. ''I've been trying to guess all the way over here.''

''I'd like your opinion on something. As you know, we lost quite a few paintings in the fire.''

"That's so sad, but you still have a wonderful collection."

"Yes, but it has been diminished. I'd like to fill the gaps with works by some of the more modern artists such as Gauguin, Monet and of course Van Gogh."

"You have good taste." Suzanna smiled. "But you'll also need patience. Their works aren't readily available. It isn't like going to a gallery and buying something by an artist who's just building his reputation."

"Have you heard of the Westbrooke collection? It isn't open to the general public, but I believe it's well-known in art circles."

"Yes, I was privileged to see it once as the guest of a curator. The Westbrooke family has been acquiring paintings for years."

"Did you know their collection is for sale?"

"No! Why would they sell? Not for the money, certainly. Henry Westbrooke is a multimillionaire."

Morgan shrugged. "People dispose of their possessions for different reasons. They might be tired of all the security problems, or perhaps they want to give more people the opportunity to enjoy the masterpieces they love."

"That's going to make one whale of an auction," Suzanna observed.

"Unless it's sold to one person. I'm considering buying it," he added casually.

She stared at him in disbelief. "Do you have any idea of how much the Westbrooke collection would cost?"

"As a matter of fact, I do."

He named an amount that almost made Suzanna choke on one of the shrimp puffs a servant had brought in earlier. "Are you *that* rich?" she blurted out before she could stop herself.

"I thought it was common knowledge—like everything else about me. I hope this won't affect our relationship." His smile had a tinge of mockery.

"It might," she admitted. "We didn't have anything in common when you were just a king. Now I *really* don't know how to talk to you. The gap is too wide to even shout across."

"I'm no different than I was five minutes ago, and you didn't have trouble then."

"I guess I was getting used to the fact that you're a king."

"You can get just as used to the fact that I'm a wealthy one. Most people don't have any problem with that," he added ironically.

"Yes, I suppose everybody wants something from you," she said slowly.

Morgan shrugged. "It comes with the territory. You can't let it bother you."

"It almost has to. How do you know if somebody is really your friend, or if they merely want a favor?"

"I don't, it's as simple as that."

"I can't believe that doesn't bother you," she said flatly.

"Let me try to explain. Everybody would like to be loved for himself alone, but sometimes people are dazzled by material things. I can't blame them, because I've never yearned for anything I couldn't have.

I've lived a life of privilege from the day I was born. How can I condemn anyone for wanting what I've always taken for granted?''

"That's remarkably tolerant of you, but with that philosophy you'd get taken advantage of a lot." Suzanna stared at him skeptically. "Somehow, I can't see you as a patsy."

He smiled. "I said I try to be understanding, not stupid. Of course I know when people are trying to manipulate me. If they're too outrageous about it, I move on."

Was that why he'd gone through so many women? Suzanna wondered. They got greedy? It might also be the reason the greatest catch on the continent was still a bachelor. He'd never been sure he was the prize, not his title and fortune.

"Don't look so pensive." Morgan laughed. "I wasn't asking for pity."

She couldn't help feeling a *little* sorry for him, but his material and physical blessings more than made up for any disappointments he might have suffered. "Anyone who can afford to buy the Westbrooke collection doesn't need pity," she said crisply. "Have you really made up your mind, or are you just thinking about it?"

"I've pretty well decided, but of course I have to wait for appraisals and documents of authenticity."

"That's very wise." Suzanna nodded. "Phony paintings and sculpture have turned up even in prestigious museums. How many pieces are in the collection? I know it's extensive."

"I have a list here, somewhere." Morgan went

over to a carved Louis XIV desk and rummaged through the litter of papers on top. "Yes, here it is. Come take a look."

Suzanna joined him and he pulled up another chair so they could sit side by side. Together, they looked at a list of famous paintings that would make any museum salivate.

"This Bonnard is my favorite!" she exclaimed, pointing to a name on the list. "The colors are glorious."

"I suppose so, but his paintings are too busy for my taste."

"How can you say that? The man was a genius!"

"Admittedly, but I prefer Gauguin. His colors are more primitive, and his strokes bolder."

"Not to mention the half-naked Tahitian beauties he painted," Suzanna teased.

"There's nothing wrong with nudity. The female body is beautiful."

"So is the male body. The ancient Greeks sculpted wonderful statues of athletes. I wonder why artists today seldom paint nude males."

"Blame the invention of the cheeseburger and French fries." Morgan grinned. "We don't have the physiques of Greek athletes anymore."

"Some of you do," she said. He wasn't the only one who'd learned from their close physical contact.

"Am I included?" he asked with amusement. "That's a nice compliment."

"It was thrown in gratis," she said lightly. "I'm one of the few people who don't want anything from you."

"That's too bad. I'd like to do a favor for you," he answered softly.

Suzanna was achingly aware of him. They were sitting within touching distance. In fact, their hands did touch briefly when they flipped the pages. And when they turned their heads to look at each other, their lips were only a whisper apart. A fact she hadn't noticed while they were discussing art.

"You can invite me to see the Westbrooke collection after you buy it," she said, quickly inclining her head to look down at the list. Pointing to a name, she said, "I could sit in front of this Degas for hours. It's my favorite."

"You just said the Bonnard was your favorite," he teased.

"Okay, so I'm fickle. I think I like one best until I see one I like better."

Something flickered in Morgan's eyes. "I thought you were different from other women."

"Everybody likes to think they're different, but I guess we all have certain similarities."

"Yes, I suppose you're right."

She smiled mischievously. "Maybe that's why your minister couldn't distinguish me from a terrorist."

"I'm still embarrassed by that," he groaned.

"Don't be, although it *was* indirectly your fault. If you'd let me change clothes first it never would have happened. I doubt if you get very many scruffy people like me wandering around these halls."

"I don't know what you mean by scruffy. You look

better than most women do when they're dressed for a fancy ball,'' he said warmly.

It was patently untrue, but nice to hear—especially delivered in that deep, honeyed voice. ''Okay, we're even now in the compliment department.''

''You mean yours wasn't true? You don't want to see me nude? I'm crushed!''

''That's not what I said,'' she protested. ''We were talking about nudity in general, and I merely mentioned that you were in good shape.''

''You sure know how to take the fun out of a compliment.'' He chuckled.

''And you certainly know how to maneuver the conversation around to sex,'' she answered tartly.

''I was merely making a point.''

''What? That men think about sex more than women?''

''I don't believe that's true. Haven't you ever fantasized about some special man? About what it would be like to lie together in a moonlit room, your bodies intertwined, his mouth tasting the sweetness of yours?''

Suzanna's pulse accelerated wildly as Morgan described the erotic scene in a smoky voice. It was a scene she'd imagined on her own, although wild horses wouldn't have dragged that out of her.

''My fantasies aren't as graphic as yours,'' she lied.

''That might be true, but at least I proved to you that there isn't such a wide gap between us, after all. You've been talking to me as if I were any other man. The same way you'd banter with that boisterous young fellow I met in your studio.''

She stared at him wide-eyed, aware that what he said was true. For the past half hour Morgan had been neither the king nor her employer, just a very stimulating companion.

"I'm right, am I not?" he asked.

"Well, partially right, anyway. Brian and I rarely have a serious conversation. He's the castle clown."

"But you felt as comfortable with me as you do with him," Morgan persisted.

"Yes, I guess I did," she said slowly.

"Splendid! I think we've made a breakthrough. We should celebrate over dinner tomorrow night." When she looked wary, he continued in a casual voice, "It's the least I can do to make up for your humiliating experience today."

"You don't have to feel obligated. I thought it was funny. At least Jablon didn't loose the dogs on me."

"Poor Suzanna. After your bad experiences here, I'm surprised you haven't taken the first flight home."

"They weren't all bad." The times she spent with Morgan would be cherished memories, she admitted to herself. "I really enjoy my work," she added hastily.

"That's not enough. I want you to be able to say you enjoyed your entire stay in Monrovia. Don't feel pressured into accepting, but I'd feel a lot better if you'd let me offer you the hospitality of the castle."

"Well, if you really want me to, I'd be delighted to have dinner with you."

"Excellent! Tomorrow night around eight, then?"

Was that a gleam of satisfaction in his eyes? Morgan really *wasn't* all that different from other men!

He thought he'd manipulated her, while actually she'd been looking for a valid reason to accept. Maybe it wasn't the wisest thing she'd ever done. His suggestive manner this afternoon would no doubt escalate tomorrow night, but he wouldn't be difficult if the answer was no.

"Eight o'clock will be just fine," she said demurely.

Morgan noticed a servant hovering in the doorway. "Yes, Paul, what is it?"

The man flicked the merest glance at Suzanna before saying, "Countess Duvain is downstairs in the drawing room, Your Highness. Shall I show her up?"

It was a jarring reminder. That redhead never seemed to be far away. Suzanna rose swiftly. "I'm always making you late for a date," she said with a bright smile.

"My time is scheduled so tightly," he said apologetically as he walked her to the door. "I have to steal an hour here and there for the things I really like to do."

Suzanna was supposed to think that meant being with her. It was a nice thought, but she didn't believe it for a moment.

"Thank you for coming," Morgan said at the door. "I'll look forward to seeing you tomorrow night."

Suzanna walked slowly back to her own wing, wondering why she felt like a balloon that had just been punctured. She certainly wasn't jealous of the countess. It wasn't as if she, Suzanna, was falling in love with Morgan.

There would be no future in such a relationship.

He lived in a royal world where commoners could visit, but not stay long.

That was no surprise. But it needn't stop her from enjoying Morgan's company tomorrow night. Her spirits rose in anticipation.

Chapter Four

Suzanna had nothing suitable to wear for dinner with a king. Who could have guessed the occasion would arise?

The only outfit she'd brought that would be borderline acceptable was a pair of lavender silk pants and a matching turtleneck pullover. If they were dressed up with heels and a string of pearls, it should look at least passable.

Suzanna took a bath instead of a shower and luxuriated in the bubbles while she looked forward to the evening. Would Morgan try to kiss her? The thought made her toes curl. He would kiss a woman with slow seduction, his lips gentle as a feather on hers at first, lighting a slow fire that would burn hotter when he parted her lips for a deeper intimacy. Her eyes were dreamy as she picked up a washcloth.

After she was dressed, Suzanna had second thoughts about her choice of an outfit. The silk knit pullover clung to her body, outlining her breasts pretty explicitly. She hadn't thought about that. But the turtleneck couldn't be called sexy. It wasn't as though she had on a blouse with a plunging neckline.

There wasn't time to change, anyway, even if she had something better to wear. She'd lingered in the tub so long, spinning silly fantasies, that she was in danger of being late.

Suzanna had just finished spraying herself with perfume when there was a knock on the door. "Oh, no!" she groaned. It could only be Brian, and she didn't want to explain the perfume and high heels. Not that there was anything wrong in what she was doing, but it was just as well not to start any gossip.

The knock sounded again while she was trying to decide on a plausible lie, but none occurred to her. Reluctantly she opened the door.

Morgan was standing in the hall, looking impossibly handsome in a dark suit and snowy linen that accentuated his deep tan. He was carrying a square white box.

Amber lights began to glow in his eyes as he gazed at her. "You look absolutely exquisite!"

She laughed self-consciously. "It's just the contrast with what I had on yesterday."

"You know that's not the reason." He handed her the box. "This turned out to be a fortuitous choice. It will match your outfit."

Suzanna opened the box curiously. Inside was a

circlet of delicate lavender orchids. "They're lovely. Thank you."

"I'm glad you like them." He took the circlet from her and slipped it on her wrist. "There, they look perfect on you. Shall we go?"

"You did say eight o'clock, didn't you?" she asked as they started down the hall. "I'm not late, am I?"

"No, you're right on time."

"Then why did you come for me? Wasn't I supposed to go to your apartment?"

"A gentleman always calls for his date."

"But you're the king. You don't pick up your date, she comes to you." That was what the countess had done last night.

"Sometimes she does, but I don't live by that rigid a set of rules." Morgan took her hand as they started down the grand staircase.

"This isn't the way to your apartment," she observed.

"I thought you'd like a change of scenery," he answered smoothly.

"Where are we going?"

"Be adventurous. Wait and see." When she looked at him doubtfully, he said with amusement, "Poor Suzanna, I'm breaking all the rules tonight. I'm sorry if that upsets you."

"I'm not upset—just annoyingly inquisitive." She gave him a mischievous smile. Suzanna suddenly realized that it didn't really matter where they went. Wherever it was, she was with Morgan and she was going to have a smashing time.

"You can arouse a lot of emotions in a man, but never annoyance," he said gallantly, squeezing her hand.

When they reached the ground floor, the sound of music came faintly from somewhere in the distance. It became louder as they walked outside onto a flagstone terrace. The music was coming from a quartet of musicians seated at a far corner of the terrace.

On the lawn a short distance away was a large white gazebo. It was lit with candles that alternately flickered and glowed like captive stars. In the center of the gazebo Suzanna could see a table and two chairs.

She turned to Morgan in delight. "Is that where we're having dinner?"

He nodded. "I thought it would be something a little different."

"You're so right! I've never had a dinner date like this before," she said happily.

"Tell me what one of your typical dates is like," he said as they strolled across the lawn.

"Oh, maybe dinner at a neighborhood restaurant and then a movie. Or if I'm going out with one of my sports-nut friends, maybe a basketball game. If the traffic is bad, which it always is, dinner could be pizza or a hot dog and beer at the game."

Morgan stared at her incredulously. "That's unbelievable!"

Suzanna laughed. "You ought to get out more and see how the other half lives. It certainly isn't like this!"

They had reached the gazebo, which looked like

something out of a fairy tale. The squat votive candles around the perimeter illuminated the lacy latticework that formed the octagonal shape of the open-air structure. A light breeze made the tiny flames dance in the darkness.

The small table in the center of the floor was as formal as any banquet table. It was covered with a cutwork linen cloth and set with the finest bone china. The service plates had a blue-and-gold border with the royal crest of Monrovia in the center, depicted in glowing colors.

Sterling candleholders held tall tapers that cast a soft light over the heavy flatwear and the floral centerpiece in the middle of the table. A cut-crystal bowl held pink roses and waxy white stephanotis that gave off a heavenly scent.

Suzanna inhaled deeply. ''Everything is so lovely. I never expected anything like this.''

''I hope you won't be disappointed that the chef didn't prepare pizza and hot dogs,'' he teased.

''That's for the typical date you asked me to describe. This certainly doesn't qualify as typical.''

He handed her a crystal flute as a servant approached with a bottle of champagne. ''What would you call tonight?''

''A very special occasion,'' she answered without having to think about it.

''That's something you only celebrate once in a while. I hope tonight is the first of many evenings like this.'' He raised his glass. ''To a lovely lady.''

Suzanna sipped her champagne, feeling a golden glow flowing through her veins. It didn't matter if

Morgan meant any of his lavish compliments. He'd put a lot of thought into this evening just to please her, and she intended to enjoy every minute of it.

"The champagne is delicious," she told him.

"I hoped you'd like it."

"Everybody likes champagne—even if they don't especially care for the taste."

Morgan looked at her in amusement. "Isn't that carrying good manners to an extreme?"

"People don't drink it just to be polite. Champagne is associated with festive events like anniversaries and weddings," she explained. "You know what I mean, happy events."

"I hope tonight qualifies," he murmured in a plush voice.

Suzanna barely heard him. She was gazing out over the beautiful setting. Acres of lush lawn surrounded the gazebo, while overhead the moon was a golden crescent in a dark blue velvet sky scattered with diamond-bright stars.

"This would be a stunning place for a wedding," she observed. "The ceremony could take place here in the gazebo, and afterward the guests could dance on the terrace and eat at tables set up on the lawn."

"If you're planning *my* wedding, I don't believe you realize the protocol that's involved."

"Yes, I suppose a royal wedding is very formal."

"That doesn't begin to describe it," he said wryly.

"I watched the royal weddings that were televised. Are yours on that grand a scale?"

"We're a much smaller country, but our rituals are

perhaps equally elaborate. The pomp and ceremony is all part of the royal proceedings. It's traditional.''

''You don't sound as though you're looking forward to it.''

Morgan shrugged. ''The people expect it, and they, after all, are the ones we're sworn to serve.''

''What was your parents' wedding like?''

''The same spectacle their parents' was, and mine will be.''

''That leaves a lot to my imagination,'' Suzanna said pointedly.

''Sometimes that's almost as enjoyable.''

''All right, I won't press you. I can tell that even discussing the subject makes you nervous.''

''Not at all. I'm not anti-marriage. I look forward to it—when I meet the right woman.''

''I hope you're spry enough to walk down the aisle when you do,'' she commented dryly.

''I think I have a few good years left in me.''

Suzanna didn't doubt that for a minute. It was impossible to imagine Morgan losing any of his vitality. He would get even more distinguished looking with the years.

''You're supposed to reassure me,'' he teased, when she didn't answer immediately.

''Okay, I think you'll make it down the aisle—as long as it isn't too far from the entry,'' she added mischievously. ''Where are your royal weddings held?''

''I'll overlook your lack of respect for your elders,'' he said with mock disapproval. ''All royal weddings from centuries back have taken place at an ancient cathedral near the center of town. Perhaps you've seen it.''

"No, I haven't had a chance to get into the city."

"That's too bad. We're very proud of our city. You really must see some of the attractions."

"I intend to." She didn't want him to get sidetracked, so she continued hurriedly, "Do you ride through the streets in those antique carriages?"

"The bride and groom arrive separately, each in a golden carriage drawn by eight horses. Her team of horses is always white, his is black. His carriage arrives first, and he steps out onto a red velvet runner embroidered with gold. It covers the stairs and continues inside, the full length of the cathedral all the way to the altar. Is that the sort of thing you want to hear?" Morgan asked.

"Yes," she said with shining eyes. "What does the king wear?"

"The groom isn't always a king. The same kind of ceremony is held for a prince. In fact, that's usually the case."

Suzanna was more interested in him. "What will *you* wear?"

"That's the embarrassing part." He gave a slight laugh. "The king wears a red satin sash across his chest, decorated with all of the ceremonial medals of Monrovia."

"That doesn't sound embarrassing. It sounds distinguished. Ambassadors wear that sort of thing on state occasions."

"They don't carry a golden scepter and wear a long velvet cloak decorated with bands of white ermine."

"It sounds like something out of an illustrated fairy tale!" she exclaimed. "Will you also wear your crown?"

"One of them. It's the official crown of Monrovia, worn only on solemn occasions."

"What does it look like?"

"It's large, gold and heavy," he answered succinctly. "Actually it's quite impressive," he admitted when she looked disappointed. "The gold is set with all the precious gems—diamonds, emeralds, rubies and sapphires. The largest of the jewels, the centerpiece of the crown, is a massive diamond supposedly presented to the ruler of Monrovia centuries ago by an Indian raja."

"It must be magnificent! Does the queen get a crown, too?"

"Nothing quite as glitzy, I'm afraid. You'll have to remember that the Souverain dynasty goes back many hundreds of years, before women made their influence felt."

"Well, at least she got a crown. What does it look like?"

"It's quite nice." Morgan described a smaller crown with a circlet of diamonds around the top and bottom, the part in between studded with the same precious stones as the king's, only not as large.

"Wow!" Suzanna exclaimed. "I'd say that's more than 'nice.' I can't imagine any woman being disappointed."

"If any of them were, it was unfortunate. The crown isn't returnable—not even for credit on another one." He smiled.

"They obviously didn't have charge cards in those days. Does the bride wear her crown when she walks down the aisle?"

"No, the groom places it on her head at the conclusion of the ceremony. If she's wise she doesn't wear high heels, because the proceedings are lengthy."

"I'm sure no bride would mind. Does he kiss her?"

"You really want all of the details, don't you?" Morgan chuckled.

"Every single one. Does he?"

"Not in front of the guests. That comes later—and I can't give you those details. You'll have to imagine them for yourself. All I can say is, the wedding night was the same then as now. Human nature hasn't changed over the centuries."

"I wasn't fishing for that kind of information," Suzanna said reprovingly.

"Don't you want to hear that royalty is human?" he asked in amusement. "Where do you think all the little princes and princesses come from?"

"I'm aware of the facts of life," she said tartly. "They just aren't the kind of details I was looking for."

"I was only trying to satisfy your curiosity. What else can I tell you?"

"What happens after the ceremony—and before they do what comes naturally," she added hastily. "Surely they don't go right from the church to his chambers."

"That's a brilliant idea. I'll have to propose it, but

I doubt if it will fly. After the ceremony the bride and groom walk down the aisle together, with two or three little girls holding up the queen's train. My mother's train was ten feet long. Her wedding pictures show that it was attached to a circlet of white orchids and orange blossoms on top of her head.'' Morgan's laughing expression turned to sadness. ''She was very beautiful,'' he said softly.

Suzanna didn't know what to say, so she reached out and touched his hand.

Morgan squeezed it tightly for a moment before continuing. ''The newlyweds get into the bridal carriage, an open carriage completely covered with flowers of every color, roses and carnations, speckled lilies, orange blossoms and more.''

''My goodness, what a spectacle!''

''Yes, a royal wedding takes months of preparation. The people look forward to it.''

''I'll bet they're getting a little impatient waiting for you to choose a bride,'' Suzanna joked.

Morgan answered her seriously. ''It isn't a choice that should be made lightly. My marriage has to last forever.''

She realized it was a touchy subject. He was willing to talk about other royal weddings, but not his own. ''To get back to that floral carriage,'' she said, rather awkwardly. ''Where does it take the happy couple?''

''All over the city. The new queen holds an armload of long-stemmed red roses. As they drive around, she throws one rose at a time to the crowd lining the streets. Out his side of the carriage, the king throws gold coins.''

"Once they find out which side he's sitting on, I'll bet everybody crosses over to the king's side of the street,'' Suzanna remarked.

"Not necessarily. A smile from a beautiful woman is more precious than gold.''

"You'd have trouble selling that one to the average man.''

Morgan trailed a finger down her cheek. "You're too young to be so cynical.''

"I'm not cynical, just a realist.'' She laughed breathlessly, her cheek tingling from his light touch.

"If that were true, how could you be so interested in what you describe as a fairy-tale wedding?''

"Even realists like fairy tales. It's called escapism.''

"I don't think you're as pragmatic as you pretend. I think you're really a closet romantic.''

"You're right,'' she finally admitted. "There are some situations nobody could resist. What woman wouldn't want to ride in a flower-bedecked carriage and dance with a king at the ball afterward? It's the ultimate Cinderella story.''

"I don't happen to have a carriage handy, and this isn't a grand ballroom, but the king of Monrovia would be honored if you would dance with him.'' He extended a hand to her.

"Miss Bentley accepts with pleasure.''

Suzanna put her hand in his and let him lead her onto the grass. The musicians switched to a waltz as if on cue. The whole thing seemed like a lighthearted dream until Morgan took her in his arms. Then he became achingly real.

His potent masculinity was like an aphrodisiac. It took great effort not to twine her arms around his neck and run her fingers through his crisp dark hair.

Morgan didn't make it any easier. He drew her closer and brushed his lips across her temple. "Sweet Suzanna, I'd like to fulfill all of your fantasies."

"You already have," she murmured.

"Then I'd like to fulfill mine." He gazed down at her with a melting smile.

She forced herself not to react, knowing Morgan would kiss her if she showed the slightest willingness. Part of her said, go for it! But another part remembered that old lecture about playing with fire.

Morgan watched the conflict play across her expressive face. He cradled her head on his shoulder and stroked her long hair. "Don't worry, little one, I won't ever pressure you into doing anything you don't want to do."

She gazed up at him, choosing her words carefully. "You're a very charismatic man."

"That's usually followed by a but." He grinned. "I'll save you the discomfort. I believe our dinner is being served." He led her back to the gazebo without a hint of annoyance.

Their first course was already on the table—jellied consommé flavored with sherry. It was served in thin china bowls and accompanied by cheese straws so flaky they melted in her mouth.

Suzanna commented on the fact. "These cheese straws are heavenly! I don't even want to think about how much butter went into them, but I'd like to know."

"I can easily find out for you," Morgan said. "Do you like to cook?"

"I do when I have the time, which isn't too often because I usually work long hours. Sometimes on the weekends I have people over for dinner, but certainly nothing this fancy. I make a big pot of spaghetti, or perhaps lasagna and tossed green salad. People congregate in the kitchen and fix their own drinks."

"It sounds like fun," he commented.

"It is, but I'll trade it for this any day." Suzanna was looking down at her plate, so she didn't notice the expressionless way he was gazing at her.

If her answer displeased him, she wasn't aware of it. Morgan was a perfect host. They talked throughout dinner like old friends. Suzanna never got the feeling that he was a man on the make. It was the best possible scenario, but perversely, she was slightly disappointed. It wouldn't have been so terrible if he'd been just a tiny bit more romantic.

The rest of the dinner was equally delicious. Without disturbing their conversation, the unobtrusive waiters served a chicken dish that looked like an illustration in a gourmet magazine.

Suzanna tasted hers and said, "Mmm, divine!"

"Do you want this recipe, too?" Morgan laughed.

"No, thanks. I never make any dish that calls for more than three ingredients."

He glanced down at his plate. "Would this be difficult to make?"

"Not if you have the right equipment—one servant

to sauté the chicken, another to wash the mushrooms and slice the onions, and a third person to go down to the wine cellar for a bottle of sherry.''

"You see? Cooking isn't so hard.'' His eyes sparkled with merriment. "You women make a big deal out of nothing.''

While they were waiting for dessert, a squirrel came to the edge of the gazebo and stared at them with bright, inquisitive eyes.

"He's a cheeky little devil, isn't he?'' Morgan said indulgently.

"He's obviously used to people,'' Suzanna said as the squirrel sidled closer. She tossed it a piece of roll, saying, "You should have been here sooner. All the choice stuff is gone.''

"You're very good with animals,'' Morgan observed as the squirrel scampered to within a foot of her.

"They seem to know when people like them.''

"How do you feel about horses?''

"I always wanted a horse, but my parents put their foot down. They were afraid I'd sneak it into my bedroom after they went to sleep.''

"I didn't know you were that kind of a girl,'' Morgan said jokingly.

"Believe it! I was a real pushover—for anything that had four feet and a tail.''

"You must see my horses. I'm very proud of them.''

"You have a racing stable, don't you?''

"Yes. I like to think they're among the finest horses in the world. My father started the stable, but

I've added to it and acquired championship breeding stallions. Some of their offspring have won world-class races." Morgan's face became animated as he talked.

Suzanna wondered a little wistfully if he ever felt that intense an interest in a woman. "It must be exciting to have your own horse in a race," she commented.

"There's nothing quite like it. They all have the potential to win, but usually one horse stands out above all the others."

"It's the same in life. Some people seem to walk around with a spotlight over their heads."

"But the glitzy people aren't always the ones you want to be with." His smile became suddenly intimate as he gazed into her eyes.

"They never seem to lack company," Suzanna commented dryly.

He shrugged. "There are a lot of reasons for popularity. The important things are character and good breeding."

"I don't know whether you're talking about horses or people." She laughed. "No, don't tell me. I'd be crushed to be upstaged by a horse."

"You have nothing to worry about. You'd be the jewel in any man's crown," he said in a husky voice.

"I'll bet you feel the same way about your favorite horse," she joked, to hide her pleasure at the lavish compliment. "What is his name?"

"His official name is Reigning Monarch, but we all call him Champ." Morgan looked at her thoughtfully. "Since you're so interested in horses and tomorrow is Saturday, how would you like to go riding?''

"I'm afraid I gave you the wrong impression," she said. "I'm accustomed to the regular horses you rent from a livery stable. I'm not skilled enough to ride a racehorse."

"Don't worry, that wasn't what I was proposing. Nobody rides Reigning Monarch but his jockey and his exercise boys. The racehorses have their own stable in the countryside, but we have a riding stable here on the grounds. I was suggesting that we take a couple of those horses along a bridal path near here. Would you like to do that?''

"I'd love to." Suzanna had given up worrying about what anyone would say. She enjoyed Morgan's company tremendously and it was nobody's business but her own.

"Splendid! How does ten o'clock sound?"

"That sounds fine." Something occurred to her. "I don't have a riding habit. Will it be okay if I wear jeans?''

"I'm sure the horse won't mind." Morgan smiled. "You'll need boots, though. What size do you wear? I'll have one of the grooms locate a pair for you."

The waiter brought a silver coffeepot to fill Suzanna's cup, but she indicated that she'd had enough. The man had also served dessert, which she'd barely touched.

"You haven't eaten your chocolate mousse," Morgan observed. "Would you prefer something else?"

She shook her head. "It was delicious, but I'm absolutely stuffed. I ate everything but the design on the plate.''

"It's refreshing to meet a woman who actually enjoys her food. So many women just pick at a lettuce leaf like a listless rabbit.''

"I could never be accused of that. My problem is that I like everything—with the exception of calamari.''

"I'll tell the chef to ban it from the menu.'' Morgan looked up as the waiter filled his coffee cup. "We won't require anything else, Pierre. You and Henri can go now.''

"You should let those poor musicians go, too,'' Suzanna said. "They've been playing for hours, almost nonstop.''

A little smile curved his firm mouth. "If I didn't know better, I'd think you wanted to be alone with me.''

"It wouldn't do me any good if I did,'' she answered matter-of-factly. "There is probably a platoon of guards out there, all watching your every move.''

"Whatever gave you that idea?''

"Personal experience.''

"The incident that night was an unfortunate misunderstanding. Guards do patrol the grounds, but I don't have bodyguards with binoculars trained on me every minute. That would be a terrible way to live!''

"I guess you get so used to it that you don't think about it anymore.''

"Come with me.'' Morgan stood and extended his hand to her. "We're going to walk around the grounds and look behind every bush and tree. I'll prove to you that there's no one out there spying on us.''

''It doesn't really matter. We aren't doing anything they shouldn't see.''

''That's no guarantee for the future,'' he said mischievously.

''Promises, promises,'' she scoffed as they strolled onto the lawn.

''Be careful about issuing a challenge, little one,'' he answered softly. ''I just might take you up on it.''

''Not until you prove we don't have an audience.''

''I'd hate that as much as you would.'' He curled his hand around the nape of her neck and stroked the soft skin behind her ear. ''Lovemaking should be a private affair between two people who want to bring each other joy.''

The moonlight made Morgan's eyes incandescent. Suzanna was hypnotized by the glow and by the sensuous feel of his fingers slowly caressing her neck. It didn't take much imagination to picture the joy he could bring her.

''You're so exquisite.'' His low voice was almost unbearably arousing. ''I'd like to kiss you everywhere and hold you in my arms all night.''

The thought was irresistible. It blossomed in her mind until she could almost feel his warm mouth on her skin. Her lips parted and his head dipped toward her, blotting out the moon and the stars, everything but him.

Suzanna wondered afterward if they would have made love there and then. She would never know, because something rustled in a nearby tree. The unexpected sound startled her and broke the spell. Her dreamy expression vanished and she moved back.

"You've made a friend," Morgan said wryly, gazing after the squirrel that had scampered down the tree trunk and disappeared into the darkness. "It's following you."

"You don't know that it's the same one. Squirrels all look alike," Suzanna said with a shaky laugh.

"I'm going to evict this one. It has a lousy sense of timing!"

She couldn't help but agree, even though she knew it was for the best. Morgan was too experienced for her. He knew how to push all the right buttons to make her forget she didn't want to get involved.

"Shall we continue our tour of the grounds?" he asked, as if nothing had happened.

Strictly speaking, nothing had, but Suzanna's nerves were still vibrating. "We can go back now. You've convinced me that we're alone." She smiled weakly.

"You're too trusting. What if the guards are all taking a coffee break?"

"Then if I were you, I'd fire them. They're not doing their job."

"Well, let's continue our stroll anyway. It's too nice a night to go in."

Morgan had a knack of putting her at ease. Suzanna always forgot her constraint in just a few minutes and found herself chatting quite naturally with him. The only thing that kept her pulse rate higher than normal was their twined fingers. He held her hand as they continued around the grounds, but it seemed like such an innocent gesture that she didn't like to object.

The grounds were fairly dark, since they were lit mainly by moonlight. But when they rounded a corner of the castle, there was a gleam of blue in the distance.

"What is that patch of blue?" Suzanna asked.

"It's the swimming pool," Morgan told her.

"I didn't know you had one. The pictures I've seen of the castle didn't show it."

"That's because photographers only like to take pictures of things that are centuries old, like the castle. My father had the pool installed when we boys were small."

When they reached the pool Suzanna exclaimed with pleasure. "This is charming! It looks like a lake you might come across in a woodland setting."

A waterfall at the deep end of the free-form pool cascaded over large rocks before splashing into the water. And instead of flagstone or brick, the pool was surrounded by grass and tropical foliage. The flowers that added color to the greenery looked as though they'd grown there in the wild, instead of being planted by gardeners.

"Would you like to go swimming?" Morgan asked as she knelt down to dabble her fingers in the water. "The air is a little cool, but the water is always kept warm."

"That's a tempting idea, but it's too far to go back to my room for a bathing suit."

"We can go skinny-dipping," he suggested with a grin.

"I never skinny-dip on a first date."

He spread his jacket on the ground for her to sit on, then sat on the grass facing her. "I don't suppose you could consider this our second date—or even our third?"

"When did we do all this dating?" she asked in amusement. "I'm sure I would have remembered."

"Well, perhaps they weren't exactly dates, but we did have a drink together on one occasion, and iced tea on another, if I remember correctly."

"Both those times could be considered business meetings."

"It was worth a try." He chuckled.

"Your effort is duly noted, but let's just enjoy this lovely setting." She leaned back on her elbows and lifted her chin to gaze up at the moon.

"Be careful. I wouldn't want you to fall back and hit your head on the edge." He snaked an arm around her shoulders for insurance.

"I'll admit I've had some mishaps, but I'm not *that* clumsy."

Her laughter died as they stared into each other's eyes. The sexual tension between them that had been just under the surface all evening now flared openly. The naked desire on Morgan's face was echoed by the small flames that licked at her midsection.

"Darling Suzanna." His arms tightened around her. "You're so adorable. I can't resist you."

His mouth hovered over hers, leaving no doubt about his own passion, but letting her make the decision. How could she deny something she wanted so desperately? With a sigh of anticipation, she clasped her arms around his neck.

Morgan's mouth closed over hers with a low sound of satisfaction deep in his throat. Suzanna uttered her own cry of delight as he parted her lips and deepened the kiss. She ran her hands restlessly over his broad shoulders as if to reassure herself that this wasn't a dream.

He lowered her gently to the ground and leaned over her, staring down with smoldering eyes. "You're so responsive. I want to make love to you a hundred different ways."

Suzanna tensed as he stroked her breast. She drew in her breath sharply when he dipped his head and kissed her hardened nipple. The sensation, even through layers of cloth, was electrifying. She wanted to tear off her clothes so she could feel his warm mouth on her bare skin. The force of her desire was frightening. She hadn't known she could feel such passion.

Staring up at him uncertainly, she said, "I don't think…" Her voice trailed off.

"Darling girl, I would never hurt you." He leaned down to kiss her sweetly. "I want you, but you have to feel the magic, too. You do want me, don't you, Suzanna?"

"Yes," she whispered. It was useless to deny something that was so obvious.

"Then don't fight it, sweetheart. I want to bring you more pleasure than you've ever known."

She couldn't think straight with his low, musical voice promising unlimited delight, and his lean body reinforcing the promise. When he trailed a line of tantalizing kisses down her cheek she turned her head restlessly, trying to capture his mouth.

The kiss they exchanged was scorching in its intensity. Morgan gathered her close and scissored one leg over both of hers. Their bodies were joined so closely that they were almost fused together, but it still wasn't enough. She wanted to feel the full male power of this irresistible man.

"My passionate little beauty," he said huskily as his hands cupped her bottom and urged her against the juncture of his thighs. "We're going to be so good together."

"I know," she murmured, tracing the shifting muscles in his back.

When Morgan slipped his hand under her pullover, Suzanna moved sensuously, welcoming his touch. There was no turning back. The sexual attraction between them had been apparent from the beginning and it had led inexorably to this moment.

The things Morgan was murmuring in her ear were so arousing that Suzanna didn't hear the sound of dogs barking. She became aware of them only when Morgan raised his head and swore pungently under his breath.

When she realized what was happening, she scrambled to her feet and hurriedly tried to straighten her clothes before the guard with the patrol dogs got there.

"I'm sorry, angel. I'll get rid of them." Morgan reached out to smooth her tumbled hair, but she stepped back.

A powerful flashlight was suddenly trained on them and a man's voice demanded, "Who's there? Come out with your hands up!" Then he recognized Morgan, and his belligerence vanished. "I'm sorry, Your Highness. I didn't know it was you."

"That's all right, Bruno," Morgan said. "We just came out for a little stroll."

The man felt more of an apology was necessary. "I heard noises, and I came to investigate."

"I understand. You were just doing your job. Everything is all right, so you can go now."

"Yes, sir, thank you, Your Highness."

It was very quiet after Bruno whistled to the dogs and left. Morgan walked into the shadows where Suzanna was standing and tried to take her hands, but she moved away.

"I suppose this means you don't want to resume where we left off," he joked, to put her at ease.

"I have to leave," she said in a muted voice.

"You have nothing to be embarrassed about," he said gently. "What happened between us was spontaneous and natural."

"Maybe to you. Sex isn't something I indulge in casually. At least, not usually," she added, since her recent behavior indicated differently.

"I didn't seduce you, Suzanna," he said quietly. "Our desire was mutual, and to me, quite beautiful."

"I'd prefer not to talk about it if you don't mind."

"I think we *should* talk, but perhaps not when you're this upset."

"You don't understand. I don't want to talk about it *ever!*"

"I see." His handsome face was austere in the moonlight. "I can only say I'm sorry I put you in this position. I've never used my title to take advantage of a woman before."

"It doesn't have anything to do with the fact that you're a king."

"Isn't that why you accepted my invitation to dinner tonight? You didn't feel you could turn me down?"

"No! I *wanted* to come, and I had a wonderful time until... well, until things got out of hand."

"That's a pretty pallid way of describing those few moments of heaven." He smiled.

She couldn't let herself think about just how heavenly they'd been! "I shouldn't have accepted your invitation. I knew I was playing out of my league, but I thought I could handle it. Obviously I couldn't."

"If you think my league means total promiscuity, you're wrong. I'll admit I've had relationships, but they've been meaningful and lengthy, not one-night stands."

"Like this one?" Suzanna asked bitterly.

Morgan sighed. "How can I convince you that you're wrong about everything? You're a very special person."

When he lifted her hand to his lips, she pulled it away hurriedly. She'd already had one lesson tonight in how seductive he could be.

"I have to go now." Before Morgan could stop her, she turned and literally ran across the lawn, back the way they'd come.

Suzanna was breathless by the time she reached her

room. How had she allowed something like this to happen?

When she thought of how she'd fallen into Morgan's hands like a ripe plum, Suzanna paced the floor distractedly.

It took a long time until she was calm enough to undress and get into bed. But even after the light was out she kept seeing Morgan's face. Worse than that, she relived the experience of their bodies molded together while his mouth set her on fire.

Nothing blotted out the erotic memories. She tossed and turned, willing herself to go to sleep, but it was almost morning before she finally dozed off.

Chapter Five

Suzanna was asleep the next morning when a knock at the door woke her. "Go away," she muttered drowsily without opening her eyes.

The knock sounded again a few moments later, fully awakening her. Now the memory of last night came rushing back and she put her head in her hands and groaned.

"I'm not up yet," she called, when the raps persisted. "Go away."

Then it occurred to her that the doors were too thick for the person on the other side to hear her. Suzanna didn't want to talk to anyone, but she'd have to get up and open the door or they'd keep coming back. She reluctantly got out of bed and put on a robe.

A liveried servant was waiting patiently in the hall

when she finally opened the door. He handed her a shoe box. "His Highness sent me to give you this, Miss Bentley."

She stared at the box with a puzzled frown, until she realized it must contain the pair of riding boots Morgan had promised her. "Tell His Highness that I no longer require these," she said coldly.

The man's face was impassive. "I was told to deliver them to you." As she was about to send an even firmer message, he said, "I was also instructed to show you the way to the stable."

"You're joking! If Morgan thinks for one minute that I—" She stopped abruptly, trying to contain her temper. The last thing she wanted was for gossip to spring up about her and the king. Morgan provided the servants with plenty to talk about without adding her to their list! Taking a deep breath, she said, "Will you please tell His Highness that I overslept this morning, so I won't be able to keep our business appointment."

"I will wait here until you're ready," the man said implacably.

"I don't *want* you to wait! I want you to go back to the king and tell him—" Once more, Suzanna had second thoughts.

She didn't know if this was Morgan's revenge for last night, but whatever his motive, he wasn't going to let her off the hook so easily. He was perfectly capable of coming over here for a showdown—the last thing she wanted where the people she worked with might overhear them.

"I'll be ready as soon as possible," she told the man curtly.

Suzanna raced into the bathroom to brush her teeth and splash water on her face. Then she flew around the bedroom, pulling on jeans and a T-shirt and brushing her hair. The angry color in her cheeks made blush unnecessary, she thought ironically.

Finally she opened the shoe box and found a new and very expensive pair of calf riding boots. Morgan must have sent a servant out to buy them early this morning. Was she supposed to be impressed? She'd be a lot more grateful if he'd just leave her alone. After putting the boots back in the box, she laced up a pair of sneakers.

Suzanna was ready in record time, figuring she might as well get the ordeal over with. Opening the bedroom door, she gritted her teeth and said to the servant, "Okay, lead the way."

Morgan was talking to one of the grooms when they reached the stable. They were both examining a spirited black stallion that kept dancing sideways and tossing his head. Morgan held the bridle and talked to the horse in a low, soothing voice that the animal gradually responded to.

He was equally good with horses and women, Suzanna thought caustically. Even though the stallion couldn't appreciate the stunning picture Morgan made, with the sun gilding his dark hair and emphasizing his patrician cheekbones. He was wearing a cotton shirt with the sleeves rolled up, and jeans that clung to his long legs and lean hips like a second skin, leaving no doubt about his masculinity. Not that Suzanna needed a reminder.

When he turned and saw her, Morgan smiled. ''There you are.'' He glanced at the box she was carrying. ''Didn't the boots fit?''

''I don't know. I didn't try them on,'' she said evenly.

''Why not?'' After noticing the hesitant glance she gave the groom, he suggested they go outside.

Once they were out of hearing, Morgan said, ''We have to talk about last night, Suzanna.''

''I'd prefer to forget it,'' she replied, looking off into the distance. ''What happened was a mistake.''

''Obviously, if you feel this way. I thought it was a lovely moment between two people who were expressing their feelings spontaneously. Evidently I was wrong and I apologize for the misunderstanding.''

''It wasn't solely your fault,'' she said grudgingly. ''I never should have accepted your invitation in the first place.''

His face was impassive. ''Because of my reputation as a womanizer?''

''That wasn't what I meant!'' She struggled to explain herself without revealing how attracted she was to him. ''I'm grateful to you for going to so much trouble to make last night special for me. Your lifestyle is as glamorous as I imagined it would be, and you made me feel I was part of it. When we sat by that lovely pool in the moonlight, I suddenly lost contact with reality.''

''Let me get this straight. You couldn't make love with me because I'm royalty and you're not?''

That wasn't the whole story, but it was close enough, Suzanna thought. "Let's just say I don't usually get caught up in a fantasy."

"You're very unusual. Many women find my title an incentive," Morgan said dryly.

"Their values are peculiar."

"Well, at least I'm glad we straightened out this whole misunderstanding. Now there's no reason why we can't be friends."

"I don't know if that's possible," she answered doubtfully.

"I'd be sorry to think you didn't trust me, Suzanna. I promise that from now on, nothing will happen that you don't want to happen."

She suddenly realized she could scarcely refuse to be friends. It would be tantamount to telling him she didn't believe he'd keep his word. But the situation didn't seem too unbearable this morning. Before she could answer, the groom appeared.

"The horses are saddled and ready to go, Your Highness," he said.

"I'll be there in a moment, but Miss Bentley has changed her mind," Morgan told the man. "You can unsaddle her mount."

"I don't want to ruin your day," Suzanna said quickly. "I'll ride with you."

"I don't mind riding alone. I only have time for a short ride, anyway." Morgan glanced at his watch. "We'd be getting a later start than I planned, and I have an appointment soon. Perhaps we can do it some other day."

"Yes, that would be nice." Suzanna couldn't believe how disappointed she was, knowing there would never be "some other day." She could recognize a brush-off. Well, what did she expect?

As she turned to leave, Morgan said, "I almost forgot. You only have the weekends free. Maybe we could reschedule our ride for tomorrow. Unless you have other plans, of course."

"No, I hadn't made any plans yet," she said breathlessly.

"Good. Then shall we say tomorrow at the same time? I have to be back by early afternoon, but that will give you time for other things, too."

Suzanna was too pleased to dwell on the fact that Morgan had another date. That was for the best, she assured herself. She still didn't want to get involved with him, but it would be nice to be on friendly terms. There was no denying that the man was good company.

Suzanna arrived at the stable before Morgan the next day. "Good morning," she called gaily as he came striding across the lawn.

"I'm sorry I'm late," he apologized.

"You aren't. I came on down because I was up early. Your nights are a lot busier than mine." When she realized how that sounded, she added quickly, "I mean, I know what an active social life you lead." That didn't sound a lot better, she thought hopelessly.

Morgan was looking at her in amusement when a servant carrying a picnic basket joined them. He stood there silently, awaiting instructions.

"You can mount up, Ben," Morgan told the man.

"I ordered a picnic lunch," Morgan explained to Suzanna. "I don't know about you, but fresh air and exercise always makes me hungry."

As he led her to their waiting horses, she wondered if Morgan had arranged for the servant to accompany them so she wouldn't think he planned any hanky-panky in the woods. That was really going a little overboard, but she'd brought it on herself.

Morgan's mount was the spirited black stallion. He'd chosen a more docile horse for her, a lovely tan mare that still managed to keep up when Morgan's horse broke into a gallop.

It was an exhilarating ride through the countryside. A bridle path wound in and out of trees and lush vegetation, alternating with meadows dotted with clover. The time flew by. Suzanna could scarcely believe it was lunchtime when Morgan dismounted in a small glade and tethered his horse to a tree. Not long afterward, the servant with the lunch basket came plodding into the clearing.

"That poor man has had to follow us all morning," she remarked.

Morgan shrugged. "I'm sure he's enjoying it more than his usual duties. Let's see what there is for lunch." As they strolled over to where the servant had spread out a cloth and was opening containers, Morgan said, "Did they include a lunch for you as I ordered, Ben?"

The man looked up with a wide grin. "Yes, Your Highness, a very tasty one."

"That's good. Shall we serve ourselves?" Morgan asked Suzanna.

"That's what we do at home," she said. "I have no idea what your version of a picnic is like."

"Aren't they more or less all alike?"

She looked at the embroidered cloth and linen napkins with the royal monogram. Spread out on the cloth was a china platter that held individual game hens roasted to a golden brown and garnished with sour *cornichons*. Other plates held rolled sandwiches, an assortment of raw vegetables artfully cut into flower shapes and a selection of fresh fruit and fancy cookies for dessert. Nearby was a silver cooler holding a bottle of white wine. Poor Ben had had to carry all this in his saddlebags.

Suzanna turned to Morgan with a dimpled smile. "Yes, I guess picnics are all pretty much alike."

They talked easily as they sat on the grass and ate with hearty appetites. Afterward, Morgan stretched out under a tree, watching Suzanna make chains out of the daisies that grew all around.

When she wove a finished circlet through her long raven hair, he smiled. "You look like a wood nymph."

"If wood nymphs wore jeans."

"Actually I think they ran around in the forest nude."

"That couldn't be right. Between insect bites and poison ivy, I'm sure they'd all have moved to the city." It was a mark of how comfortable they felt with each other that they could joke like this, Suzanna thought happily.

After Ben had packed up the remains of the picnic, Morgan sent him back to the castle. "Shall we forge on?'' he asked Suzanna, rising and walking over to untie the horses.

She was ashamed of her momentary suspicion that Morgan was arranging for them to be alone. Of course he'd sent the man back! Ben had followed them for a reason, and that reason was no longer valid.

The scenery changed after a while. The trail led up a fairly steep hill that overlooked the surrounding countryside. When they reached the top, Morgan dismounted.

''Come with me. I want to show you something.'' He walked her over to the edge of the promontory and put his arm around her shoulders.

Suzanna tensed and turned her head to look at him, but Morgan's attention was on the scene below. His face, in profile, was like a Greek god's, the same clean lines and strong features. Her gaze lingered on his mouth, remembering its firmness on her own.

''Isn't that a beautiful sight?'' He hugged her closer in his enthusiasm.

She turned her head reluctantly and looked where he was pointing with his free hand.

The cliff looked down on a winding stream. The clear water below was rushing over rocks, foaming with the effort as it turned and twisted between its narrow banks.

''What a charming sight,'' Suzanna said, shaking off Morgan's spell. ''It's so picturesque.''

''I thought you'd like it. This is one of my favorite spots.''

''I had no idea Monrovia was so beautiful.''

"You sound surprised. You should get out of the castle and see some of our attractions."

"I'd like that," she murmured.

"I'll give you a list of my favorite places. When you have some free time, just call the steward's office and tell him when and where you want to go."

"I'll do that," Suzanna said, masking her disappointment that Morgan didn't offer to take her himself. "You certainly provide great fringe benefits."

"I like to keep my people happy—one way or another," he drawled, before walking over to untie the horses.

When they were mounted once more, Morgan looked at his watch. "We'd better start back. I didn't realize it was getting so late."

At least she'd made him forget about his date for a while, Suzanna told herself. That made her feel better for some reason.

Suzanna didn't know when or if she'd hear from Morgan again. He hadn't even hinted at a future date when they returned from their ride. Or if not a date, some kind of meeting, even if it was just a drink after work. He had obviously lost interest in her. *Get over it!* she told herself impatiently.

Suzanna had accepted the fact that her brief glimpse into the royal way of life was over. She was immersed in her work when Morgan's low, husky voice from the doorway made her heart skip a beat.

"I didn't expect to see you again!" she blurted out.

"Why not? I live here." He smiled.

"I meant, I know how busy you are," she answered coolly, recovering her poise. "I didn't think you'd have time to keep tabs on the restoration work."

"As I once told you, I like to know everything that's going on. How is the work coming along?"

She gave him a progress report and they chatted briefly, then he left.

This happened several times. Morgan was always friendly and relaxed, but their conversation never became personal. That's why Suzanna was surprised when he varied the routine one day.

"I never got around to asking if you like opera," Morgan remarked casually.

"Yes, very much," she said. "My parents started taking me at an early age. On special occasions we'd take a train to New York and go to the Metropolitan Opera House."

"Our opera house isn't as grand, but we're quite proud of it. A group of us are going to a performance tomorrow night. Would you care to join us?"

"Tomorrow night!" Suzanna exclaimed. "I don't see how I can."

Morgan looked at her narrowly. Had he made a mistake by going slowly? "You have a date?" he asked.

"No, I meant I don't have anything to wear. It's probably formal, isn't it?"

He relaxed and nodded, laughing. "Why is that the first thing a woman thinks of?"

"Because some of us don't have extensive wardrobes. All a man has to do is put on a dark suit. A woman doesn't have one outfit that fits all occasions.''

''If that's the only thing that's bothering you, it's no problem. Take a car and driver and go out and buy a dress. Charge it to me.''

''I can afford to pay for my own clothes.''

''I'm only offering to buy you one dress, not a diamond bracelet,'' he said mildly.

''It's the same principle.''

''That would come as a surprise to a lot of women I know,'' he commented.

''Have you considered getting a different set of friends?'' Suzanna joked, her spirits soaring. It had just sunk in that Morgan had asked her for a date! ''I'll take you up on your offer of transportation to the city. If I can find a dress, I'd love to go to the opera with you.''

He took a card out of his pocket and scribbled something on it. ''You might try this place first. Show them this card. I've heard a lot of the ladies get their gowns there.''

Meaning Sophia, no doubt, but Suzanna didn't care. Morgan was taking *her* tomorrow night, not the redhead!

After she'd left, the king summoned his secretary. ''I want you to call Gaultiere's—it's a dress shop. Tell them I'm sending over a customer. I want them to quote eighty percent off the price of whatever they show her. If she buys anything have the shop bill me the difference.''

Morgan phoned Suzanna's room the next night to tell her the others were gathering at the castle in one of the small salons, so he would have to pick her up a little early. She chose to meet him there instead, which gave her more time to fuss over her appearance.

The gown she'd bought at Gaultiere's was perfect—and amazingly reasonable, although a lot more than she usually paid for a dress. It was a simple ice-blue sheath, unadorned except for rhinestone straps. Around her bare shoulders she draped the matching chiffon stole embroidered with clear bugle beads.

Her blue eyes sparkled like gems as she paused at the entrance to the petit salon. The others were already there—Morgan, his brother and some people Suzanna didn't know. They were all elegantly dressed, but one woman stood out from the others.

She was an older woman with white hair, beautifully arranged. Her gown was silver brocade, and she wore magnificent jewelry, all of it unquestionably real.

When Morgan turned and saw Suzanna, the expression on his face made her heart race with happiness. His eyes glittered with unmistakable desire as he glided toward her.

Raising her hand to his lips, he said in a throaty voice, "You look exquisite."

She laughed delightedly. "I'm an artist, remember? I'm used to touching up things."

"You don't need retouching. You're perfect just the way you are."

"Are you going to bring that beautiful girl in

here?'' The older woman called. ''Or do you intend to make us guess who she is?''

Morgan kept Suzanna's hand in his as he led her into the room. ''This impatient lady is my good friend Estelle Corday,'' he said, indicating the older woman.

''The head of Estelle Corday cosmetics?'' Suzanna asked incredulously. The woman was a legend! She kept a tight grip on one of the largest cosmetics companies in the world, and still found time for a glamorous personal life, hobnobbing with royalty and the entertainment world alike.

''Don't try to tell me you use my cosmetics,'' Estelle said. ''We'd go bankrupt if we had to depend on young things like you with perfect skin.''

An attractive young woman about Suzanna's age laughingly said, ''Aunt Estelle takes it as a personal affront when she sees someone who doesn't need her products.''

''This is Paulette, Estelle's niece.'' Morgan continued the introductions. ''And you know Kenneth.''

The other couple were Prince Alexis Tamarov and his wife, Princess Katrine, a distinguished-looking woman with a patrician face and a stunning figure. The prince also raised Suzanna's hand to his lips, commenting, ''Estelle is right, you *are* a beautiful girl. Morgan is very fortunate.''

''Oh, we're not… I mean, I'm his…''

As she floundered, Morgan put his arm around her shoulders and said, ''I am indeed a lucky man.'' He beckoned to a servant carrying a tray of filled cocktail glasses and said to Suzanna, ''Would you like one of these, or shall I have Henri bring you something else?"

"If those are champagne cocktails I'd love to have one," she said.

"Because you like the taste, or because this is a special occasion?" Morgan asked softly.

The reference to their ill-fated dinner date no longer bothered her. Maybe it was the dress, or more likely the acceptance by all these nice people. For whatever reason, Suzanna felt completely relaxed.

"This is definitely a special occasion," she answered happily. "How often do I get to hobnob with a king, two princes and a princess?"

"I'm glad I can satisfy your fantasies in one respect, anyway," Morgan replied satirically. He turned away to answer a question from his brother.

"I love your dress," Paulette said as Suzanna joined her and her aunt. "Did you get it here in Monrovia?"

"Yes, Morgan sent me to Gaultiere's. They have fabulous things."

"You do look smashing, my dear, and I agree that muted elegance is preferable to ostentation. But I think a little more jewelry would still be tasteful," Estelle hinted delicately.

"What Auntie is saying is, if you've got it, flaunt it." Paulette grinned.

"I might agree if I had anything to flaunt." Suzanna smiled. Her jewelry that night consisted of silver earrings and a modest silver bracelet.

"That's shocking! Why don't you give this lovely

girl some earrings and a bracelet or two?'' she asked Morgan, who had come to join them.

''I'm afraid you've gotten the wrong idea,'' Suzanna said hurriedly. ''I'm just an employee here.'' She explained briefly what her job was.

''I see,'' Estelle said thoughtfully, looking from her to Morgan. ''He must be a generous employer. Gaultiere's is ridiculously expensive.''

''That's what I was afraid of when Morgan sent me there,'' Suzanna said. ''I was sure I couldn't afford to buy anything. Their prices *are* higher than I'm used to, but certainly not what I expected.''

As Estelle's eyes met Morgan's, he changed the subject smoothly. ''Suzanna is too modest about the importance of her job. She's done some amazing restoration work.''

''I think I'd be nervous working on a priceless masterpiece,'' Paulette remarked.

''I don't let myself think about the millions of dollars involved if I goof. Not that there's the remotest possibility of that,'' Suzanna added with a laughing glance at Morgan.

''I hope that magnificent Rubens wasn't damaged in the fire,'' Prince Alexis said. He and the others had strolled over to join them. ''It was always one of my favorites.''

''I never have to worry when gorgeous women flirt with my husband. They always have marvelous figures, and Alexis prefers fat ladies,'' the princess joked, alluding to the voluptuous nudes that Rubens was famous for.

''I wouldn't say I'm partial to the well endowed,''

he said. "I chose you, didn't I, my dear? Your figure is faultless."

"Thank you for the nice sentiment, darling, but most men don't actually choose their wives. Clever women make them think they do."

"Are you listening, Morgan? You're in greater danger from predatory women than most men. You have more worldly goods to offer," Alexis said jocularly. "So, be forewarned."

"That isn't very helpful, Alexis," Estelle chided. "Morgan's people are already waiting impatiently for him to get married."

"Leave the poor man alone," Kenneth said. "Morgan will choose his queen when he finds someone suitable."

"No, he'll marry when he meets the one woman he can't imagine living without," Katrine said. "It won't be a reasoned, intellectual choice, I guarantee you."

"I'm sure we could find something more interesting to discuss than my personal life." Morgan's tone was light, but it didn't disguise his displeasure.

After a moment's awkwardness, Paulette said to Suzanna, "How long do you think it will take to restore all of the paintings?"

"Before I got here I expected it to take a matter of weeks," she answered. "Once I saw the extent of the damage, I revised my opinion to at least a couple of months."

"Will you be able to stay that long?"

"It's no problem. Morgan might get tired of having

me and the other workers underfoot, but we're all happy to be here.''

They discussed the disastrous fire and the damage to the castle. Then a short time later, Morgan announced that it was time to leave.

"The cars are waiting outside whenever you're ready," he said.

Two long stretch limousines with the royal crest emblazoned on the side were standing at the entrance. Suzanna and Morgan got into the first one, along with his brother and Paulette. The other couple and Estelle followed in the second car.

Suzanna glanced contentedly around the luxurious interior. "This car is wonderfully comfortable."

"Isn't it, though?" Paulette agreed. "I always feel so delightfully decadent when I ride around in it."

"Undoubtedly, but I could get used to that." Suzanna laughed, stroking the soft upholstery.

Morgan's face was shadowed, so she couldn't see his expression.

Their arrival at the opera house created a stir as everyone jostled for a look at the king. Then the rest of his party came in for a close scrutiny, especially Suzanna, since she appeared to be his date.

Most of the crowd merely whispered excitedly among themselves, but a couple of extroverted souls called out a greeting to the king. Morgan smiled and waved in a restrained manner as he hurried Suzanna inside.

"Now I know what it's like to be a celebrity," she said as they walked up a short flight of carpeted steps.

"It's kind of fun to have people think you're important."

"Wait till you've been staked out by the paparazzi," he said grimly. "You'll feel more like a missionary surrounded by hungry cannibals."

"Don't disillusion the girl," Estelle chided. She and the others were behind them on the stairs. "She looks smashing tonight. Naturally she's enjoying the attention she attracted."

"I'll be happy to give her all the attention she desires," Morgan commented as they entered the box.

Suzanna barely heard him. She was too busy looking at the spectacle that greeted her. Morgan had a right to be proud of his opera house. Massive crystal chandeliers hung from a lofty ceiling that was decorated with bas-reliefs touched with gold leaf. A maroon velvet curtain embroidered in gold thread was drawn across the stage, which was just below and to the right of their box.

"Let's put the ladies in the front seats so they can have an unobstructed view," Morgan suggested.

The royal box held eight small gold armchairs upholstered in wine-colored damask, carrying out the color scheme. They were arranged in two rows at present, but the chairs could be moved as desired. After seating the women by the railing, Morgan and the two men took seats behind them.

"This is fantastic!" Suzanna exclaimed. "It's the first time I've ever been able to see all of the stage. I usually have some huge man sitting in front of me."

"Or one of those windshield-wiper couples," Paulette said.

"Yes, those are definitely the worst," Suzanna agreed.

Morgan looked puzzled. "What's a windshield-wiper couple?"

"Two people who keep moving their heads back and forth so they can whisper to each other all during the performance," Suzanna explained. "You can't know what a luxury this is."

"I'm glad you're enjoying yourself," he said.

"I'm having a fabulous time!" she answered enthusiastically.

Suzanna was enchanted by the superb production of *Tosca.* She wasn't aware of anything else as she listened to the haunting music and watched the tragedy unfolding onstage. She had no idea that Morgan was intently watching her instead of the diva.

After the performance, Morgan took their little group to a restaurant for a midnight supper. They were ushered through a plush dining room filled with people in evening dress—obviously opera goers like themselves. But unlike the others, Morgan's party was shown to a private room.

During supper they discussed the opera. Opinion was divided among them on the diva's performance. Kenneth thought her voice lacked its usual clarity, while the princess disagreed. As the others argued the point, Suzanna ate her lobster Newburg without comment.

"We haven't heard from you." Alexis looked at her inquiringly. "What's your opinion of tonight's performance?"

"I thought it was superb," she answered. "I've

never enjoyed *Tosca* more, and I've seen it countless times, including at the Met in New York by internationally acclaimed artists."

"I like your enthusiasm," Estelle said approvingly. "People today are so negative about everything. It's perceived to be sophistication, but I just find it annoying."

Alexis smiled indulgently. "Nobody could accuse Suzanna of being blasé. It's a pleasure to be with someone who isn't afraid to enjoy herself openly."

"Her enthusiasm might dim if she had to endure any of those deadly dull state functions we're all forced to attend," Princess Katrine said dryly. "Morgan could tell her about those."

Suzanna smiled. "He'd find it hard to convince me."

"I'm having a party on Saturday night that I hope won't be dull," Estelle said. "It's short notice, but I'd like you to come if you're free."

"That's so nice of you. I'd love to come!" Suzanna exclaimed without thinking. Did Estelle expect Morgan to bring her as his date, just because she was with him tonight? That could be awkward for him. It might look as though they were having a relationship—which of course they weren't.

"Splendid," Estelle said. "Eight o'clock, informal dress."

"Well, uh... I just remembered something." Suzanna slanted an oblique glance at Morgan. "I'd really love to come to your party, but I forgot that I made a tentative date with some of my co-workers. I'd better check with them first."

"Surely you can change the date," he said.

"Don't pressure the girl," Estelle chided. "You don't have to give me an answer right now," she said to Suzanna. "It will be a big party. Just come if you can. I'll be delighted to see you."

While the others began to discuss parties in general and what constituted a good one, Morgan leaned closer to Suzanna. "I told you I can always tell when people aren't telling the truth. Why did you change your mind about Estelle's party?"

"I accepted without realizing she didn't consult you first. You might have wanted me to refuse."

"Why would I have any objection?"

"You could have reasons," she answered vaguely.

"I can't think of any that would give me more pleasure than spending an evening with you."

She'd given him an out, Suzanna thought happily. If he was determined to be a gentleman, why should she deny him the pleasure?

But her happiness faded when they arrived back at the castle. After the others had transferred to their own cars and driven off, Kenneth said good-night and went to his quarters. Suzanna and Morgan were alone at the foot of the grand staircase. Although it would have been the perfect ending to an enchanted evening if Morgan had kissed her good-night, he seemed distracted and asked if she minded going back to her room alone.

Suzanna walked up the stairs, feeling a little let down. Was Morgan upset about something? He was probably just tired, she told herself. But when she turned to look back from the landing, he was going out the front door.

Morgan had a problem that he needed to work out alone. He walked around the castle grounds with his hands stuffed in his pockets, thinking about Suzanna.

At first she had been just a beautiful woman he wanted to take to bed. But as he got to know her better, his emotions became more complicated. She was smart and interesting and unpretentious. That in itself was a refreshing change.

But was she really as naive as she sometimes appeared? Or was she a very clever woman with an agenda? Before this, he'd been touched by her delight in the small luxuries he took for granted. But tonight he wondered if they were more important to her than he realized.

Suzanna had even remarked on how impressed she was to be in the company of so much royalty. Then there was her pleasure at riding in a limousine and sitting in the royal box, her excitement at being taken for a celebrity. Any normal person would enjoy those things if they'd never experienced them before, he told himself. Yet he couldn't help wondering if he was making excuses for Suzanna because he didn't want to be wrong about her.

Was Princess Katrine correct? Was he following his heart instead of his head? Not that he was in love with Suzanna. It would be foolish to get involved with her—for just about every reason.

But he had no intention of getting involved, Morgan reminded himself. He simply enjoyed her company, and she seemed to enjoy his. If part of his allure was the inevitable glamour that surrounded a king, so what? They could still maintain a friendly relationship. In fact, it would be callous of him to stop seeing her. Then she'd really think his reputation as a fickle playboy was justified. The best course of action was to continue his friendship with Suzanna and stop analyzing every facet of it.

Morgan walked back to the castle, a lot more cheerful than he'd been when he'd started out.

Chapter Six

Suzanna wanted to look her best at Estelle's party so she'd gone back to Gaultiere's to buy another dress. It was perfect for the occasion, but Suzanna was all thumbs when she put on her makeup that Saturday night. It seemed to take forever to achieve the desired effect. When a knock sounded at the door she was still in her robe.

That couldn't be Morgan! Nothing had been said, but she'd taken it for granted that she'd meet him downstairs, like the last time. Maybe he'd sent a servant to remind her.

When she opened the door it was a toss-up as to who was more startled, Morgan or Suzanna. "Did you forget we had a date tonight?" he asked.

"No, I'm all ready except to put on my dress."

She clutched at the neckline of her sheer robe as he gazed at her curved figure with interest. "Come in. I'll be with you in just a minute." She grabbed her dress from the closet and disappeared into the bathroom.

When she returned in almost the promised time, Morgan had his back to her as he gazed around the room. "I only came to the door when I was here the last time. I didn't realize your accommodations were so spartan."

"I wouldn't say that. They're very comfortable."

"Perhaps I should have you moved to the west wing," he mused, looking at the clutter of objects on the small end table next to the single bed. "The rooms are much larger."

"No, don't do that!" Suzanna could just imagine how much gossip that would generate! "I never did like to commute," she joked. "This is close to my studio."

"The west wing isn't that—" Morgan stopped in midsentence when he turned and saw her. "I always think you can't look any lovelier, and then you manage to."

This time she'd settled on a pink silk dress with little cap sleeves. The only ornamentation was a flat, double bow of black silk at the point of the asymmetrical neckline.

"Thank you." His admiration made her flush with pleasure. "I went back to Gaultiere's for this."

"I know," he murmured.

"How did you know?" she asked in surprise. "I only bought it yesterday afternoon."

His sultry look vanished. "I meant to say, I could have guessed. Their gowns have a distinctive look."

"And they're so reasonable—at least, for the style and quality. I guess it has something to do with the high exchange rate at the present time. The dollar buys more overseas."

"That must be it." Morgan opened the door. "Shall we go?"

The Corday home looked like a palace. A white gravel road wound through green lawns to the imposing front entry that faced a reflecting pool with a marble statue in the center. Lights streamed from all the downstairs windows of the house, and music drifted out to linger on the breeze.

A butler greeted Morgan and Suzanna, and ushered them to the door of a long drawing room filled with people. The ones closest came over to greet Morgan. When he introduced Suzanna, she could see the speculation on their faces—the women especially. She could guess what they were thinking, but it didn't bother her. It was a heady experience to be with the most powerful and sought-after man at the party!

Soon everybody there knew the king had brought someone new, a woman they knew nothing about. Suzanna was enjoying her unexpected celebrity when they were joined by the redheaded countess.

She ignored Suzanna and kissed Morgan's cheek, then made a big production about wiping away a tiny smudge of lipstick. "Don't worry, it's just a little speck. Not nearly the amount I usually leave." She gave a throaty laugh.

Morgan's face was expressionless as he said, "You know Suzanna, of course."

Sophia looked at her blankly. "I don't believe we've met."

"Perhaps you don't recognize me standing up," Suzanna said mischievously. "The last time we saw each other I was lying on the couch in Morgan's den."

Sophia stared at her incredulously. "That was you?"

"In the flesh," Suzanna drawled.

"May I get you ladies a drink?" Morgan asked.

"Don't you think we should say hello to our hostess first?" Suzanna asked innocently. It was a polite excuse to get away from the woman. She'd underestimated the countess, however.

"Estelle is over there by the fireplace. I'm going to borrow Morgan for a few minutes." Without waiting for either of them to say anything, Sophia took Morgan's arm and pulled him away.

Suzanna told herself he didn't have a choice, but she couldn't help feeling abandoned in a sea of strangers. Suddenly she spotted a familiar face.

Paulette appeared out of the crowd. "I'm glad you could make it," she said. "Where's Morgan?"

"In one of the bedrooms, if that red-haired countess gets to choose," Suzanna answered grimly.

Paulette laughed. "You have to admire her tenacity. She's been chasing Morgan for years."

"He must have given her some encouragement."

"Not really. He's too much of a gentleman to come right out and tell her she has two chances—little and none. But you'd think she'd get the message by now.''

Suzanna looked at her doubtfully. ''You mean they really aren't... involved?''

''It's only wishful thinking on her part. They've known each other for years, and there was a period when they were, well, maybe a little friendlier.'' Paulette put it delicately. ''But that was some time ago, and I'm sure Morgan didn't make any promises he wasn't prepared to keep. He doesn't have to. Women throw themselves at him all the time. Sophia is just more blatant than the rest.''

Suzanna felt a whole lot better. She didn't want to show too much interest, however, so she simply said, ''Some women never know when to give up.''

''Especially when the stakes are so high. She isn't the only one who would like to be queen of Monrovia.'' When Suzanna gave her a startled look, Paulette laughed. ''I wasn't speaking personally. Morgan is a very sexy man, but I'm not dumb enough to fall in love with him.''

''Yes, I suppose the competition is fierce.''

''That, too, but I was referring to my unsuitability. The old men in his cabinet would have a collective heart attack if he married a commoner.''

''If the other ministers are like the one I met, they'll die of something else. I've already tangled with a man named Jablon, and I can tell you, he's too mean to have a heart.'' Suzanna's lip curled, remembering the unpleasant encounter.

''The inner circle are all like that. You'd think they invented Morgan and owned the patent on him.''

"But he's the king! They can't tell him what to do."

"They can't make him do it," Paulette corrected. "But they have a certain amount of influence over him. These men all served his father, and Morgan was brought up to respect his elders. If they approach him in the right—" Paulette paused as some people came up to greet her. She introduced Suzanna, and the conversation became general.

While they were talking, Morgan returned and took Suzanna's hand, drawing her away from the group. "I'm sorry for leaving you alone," he told her in a muted voice.

"You didn't have to worry about me," she said. "I can always find somebody to talk to."

"That isn't the point. I shouldn't have left, but…" He paused unhappily.

She could see his dilemma. He couldn't blame Sophia. It would be unchivalrous—even though her behavior had been deplorable. Suzanna might not have been this sympathetic before talking to Paulette.

Now she gave him a dazzling smile. "You can redeem yourself by getting me a drink. And then I'd really like to say hello to our hostess."

"Consider it done. I wish all my problems were that easy to solve." He put an arm around her shoulders and led her through the crowd.

"You shouldn't have any problems," she remarked. "You're the king of Monrovia. You're also rich, handsome and your hairline isn't receding."

His eyes sparkled with amusement. "Assuming

those things are true, I'm not responsible for any of them.''

''That's nothing to feel guilty about. A lot of people would be happy to change places with you.''

''I wouldn't change places with anybody tonight,'' he said in a velvet voice.

Suzanna felt weightless, as though she'd actually drifted to cloud nine. Estelle's voice punctured the dream.

''There you are,'' she called, and beckoned them over. ''I knew you were here. Everyone's buzzing about Suzanna. They want to know who she is.''

''What did you tell them?'' Morgan asked.

''I said she's the queen of Argentina.''

''They don't have a queen,'' he said.

''Don't tell anyone. You'd be surprised at how many people believed me.''

''Maybe Argentina needs a queen, but they just don't know it,'' Suzanna mused. ''I think I'll apply for the job.''

''You already have a job—with me,'' Morgan said fondly.

''But not as queen.''

His face went blank, and she wondered if he thought she was adding her name to the list of eligibles. Couldn't he tell that she was only joking?

''Not that I'd want to be queen of Monrovia, even if the job was offered to me,'' she said lightly.

''Because I'd be part of the package deal?'' Morgan asked, just as lightly.

Estelle sensed the flare of tension between them and intervened smoothly. ''The waiters must not be doing their job. Neither of you has a drink.'' She beckoned to a waiter with a tray of glasses.

''You have a beautiful home,'' Suzanna remarked.

''Thank you, my dear. You must come over when it isn't such a mob scene. Why don't you show her around?'' Estelle said to Morgan. ''The food is outside, and there's dancing in the next drawing room.''

''It would be my pleasure.'' He took two glasses off the tray a waiter was holding out, and handed one to Suzanna as Estelle left to chat with some of the other guests.

Another drawing room of equal size opened off the one they were in. The doors between the two rooms were folded back now, but they could be closed when a smaller space was desired. A portable dance floor had been laid over the carpet in the second room, and couples were dancing to music provided by a small combo.

''This looks like the setting for an operetta,'' Suzanna said as she gazed around with shining eyes. Velvet draperies were looped back from tall windows, and gold wall sconces with crystal prisms cast a soft light. ''If the women were dressed in sweeping ball gowns, it would be a peek into the past.''

''I don't believe they played rock music in those days.'' Morgan smiled. The combo was playing something loud and rhythmic.

''Use your imagination,'' Suzanna said. ''Be romantic.''

''Gladly.'' He took the glass out of her hand and set it, along with his, on a small table. As he took her

in his arms, the musicians finished the rock number
and began to play a haunting love song.

The magic between them was even stronger than
the first time they danced together. Since then, Suzanna had felt his mouth on hers, the passion in his
taut body as they lay together on the grass. When
their bodies were this close again, it was difficult to
blot out the memory.

Morgan rested his lips on her temple and made a
low sound of satisfaction. Was he remembering, too?
She looked up at him uncertainly.

He smiled. "Are you having a good time?"

"I'm having a wonderful time," she said softly.

"I'm glad. I want to make all your nights this romantic."

The light in his topaz eyes was so bright she was
dazzled by it. Suzanna looked away, afraid her vulnerability would be evident. She was only vaguely
aware of the people around them—Paulette laughing
with a young man, Sophia dancing nearby. None of
it really registered, though.

"You told me to be romantic, and when I try to
be, you give me the silent treatment," Morgan complained.

"You're trying too hard," Suzanna said lightly. "It
has to look spontaneous to be believable."

"There are limits to how spontaneous I can be in
the present circumstances. What I'd like to do and
what is acceptable in polite society are two different—" He paused as another couple came up to them
on the dance floor.

The man put his hand on Morgan's shoulder.

"Shall we change partners?" His own partner was Sophia.

Morgan gave them a smile that didn't reach his eyes. "Isn't that sort of thing reserved for high school dances?"

"Oh, don't be stuffy, Morgan!" Sophia moved toward him. "It's fun to do silly things now and then." She completely ignored his partner.

Suzanna moved out of Morgan's arms because she had no choice. It wouldn't have surprised her if Sophia had pulled her away forcibly. The redhead replaced her in Morgan's arms, and in another moment they disappeared into the crowd of dancers.

Since nobody had introduced Suzanna and the blond man, they introduced themselves. He told her his name was Theo Treville. While they were dancing she learned that he was president of his family's bank, but his passion was breeding horses.

"Is that how you know Morgan?" Suzanna asked.

"No, we've been friends and rivals for most of our lives."

"Rivals?"

"We often have horses entered in the same race."

"Oh. I thought perhaps you competed for the same women," she said carelessly.

"I wouldn't rule out the possibility," he said, gazing at her admiringly. "Are you going to be in Monrovia long? Sophia said you're working on Morgan's art collection."

"Yes, I am. There was extensive damage. I don't really know how long I'll be here."

"That's good news for Morgan—and I hope for the rest of us," he added with a winsome smile.

"That's very flattering, but you're wrong about Morgan and me. He and Sophia obviously have some kind of…understanding."

Theo followed her glance at the other couple. Sophia was whispering intimately in Morgan's ear. Her clasped arms around his neck indicated how closely their bodies were joined.

"Appearances can be deceiving," Theo said dismissively.

That was, in essence, what Paulette had said, but Suzanna was finding it increasingly difficult to swallow. She felt like telling Theo that, but she didn't want him to think Morgan's love life mattered to her.

Suzanna would have felt immeasurably better if she'd heard the conversation Morgan was having with Sophia. The countess had kept up a running chatter, reminding him of fun times they'd had together, especially a party where the drummer in the orchestra had been drunk. He'd decided to play a loud, not very expert, solo during every number, even the tender love songs.

Morgan couldn't help smiling at the recollection, although he was seriously annoyed at Sophia. "Marietta wanted to fire him on the spot," he said, referring to their hostess that night. "But he couldn't hear her through all the noise, so he kept on flailing away at the drums."

"We do have a good time together, don't we, darling?" she asked softly.

"And I hope we always will. I value your friendship, Sophia, but—"

She cut him off swiftly. "That means so much to me. You know how I feel about you, too, my love."

Morgan gritted his teeth in an effort to keep his irritation in check. "I'm sure you know what I'm saying. I've always been honest with you about our relationship."

"You just said you care about me!"

"I said we're *friends*. That doesn't give you the right to drag me away from someone I'm with whenever the whim strikes you. It was incredibly rude, and it put me in an embarrassing position."

"I assume you're referring to Miss what's-her-name, your employee," Sophia said dismissively. "Did she give you a bad time because I borrowed you for a few minutes? She should be grateful to be here tonight. I'm sure everybody was surprised that you brought her."

"I couldn't care less what anybody thinks, but for your information, she isn't the outsider you suppose. I didn't invite Suzanna to this party. Estelle did."

"How does she know Estelle?"

"That isn't important. What matters is that we understand each other. I don't expect this to happen again," he said grimly.

"Are you saying you're interested in her?" Sophia asked bluntly.

Morgan hesitated for an imperceptible instant. "She's a bright, personable lady who is also good company. But even if she weren't any of those things, I'd expect my friends to be civil to her. If you don't think you can manage to be polite to Suzanna—or anyone else I might be out with in the future—then perhaps it would be better if we went our separate ways from now on."

She gave him a startled look. "I'm sorry, Morgan. It won't happen again, I promise. Please don't cross me off your list!"

"I wasn't threatening you," he said impatiently. "I just want you to act like an adult."

"I will, believe me, I will!"

"All right, let's just forget about it."

"Can we kiss and make up?" she asked in a small voice.

"Of course." He smiled and kissed her cheek.

That was what Suzanna saw before she hurriedly turned her head.

The music stopped a few minutes later and Theo released her reluctantly. As Morgan and Sophia joined them, he said to Suzanna, "Thank you for the dance. I enjoyed it."

"I did, too." She was only being polite, but it was gratifying to see the flash of annoyance on Morgan's face.

"I hope I'll see you again," Theo said.

"I'd like that," she answered as Morgan led her off the floor.

"You and Theo seem to have hit it off quite well," he remarked casually.

"Yes, he's a very nice man. He said you two were good friends."

"We have been up until now," Morgan said dryly. "What else did he tell you about me?"

"That you both have racing stables. I'm sure your conversation with the countess was more interesting," Suzanna said evenly.

Instead of answering, Morgan took her hand and led her outside onto the patio. Tables and chairs were set up on the extensive lawn, along with a red-and-white-striped tent where a lavish buffet supper was displayed on a long table. There was also a bar, although waiters circulated among the guests, ready to bring any kind of drinks.

The guests milled around the lawn area, which was lit by tall torches spaced at intervals, but the patio was shadowed and relatively deserted. Morgan led Suzanna to a quiet corner and turned to face her.

Hemming her in loosely with a hand braced against the wall on either side of her, he said, "I didn't want Theo to cut in on us, but there was nothing I could do about it."

"I realize that," Suzanna said politely.

The lack of conviction in her voice made Morgan sigh. "Whether you believe it or not, I'm having a better time than I usually do at these affairs. Your spontaneity and open enjoyment at being here make everyone else seem jaded."

"I don't see how anyone could *not* enjoy being at a party like this. If that makes me unsophisticated, I'll just have to live with it."

"That isn't what I meant at all! I'm trying to tell you that you're a very special person, and you've made this a very special evening for me."

Suzanna was flooded with joy. Morgan didn't have to reassure her that he wasn't involved with Sophia—

which was what this was all about. He wasn't used to answering to anyone, and certainly not to her. Maybe she really was special to him?

She gave him a brilliant smile. "If you really want to see some enthusiasm, you can point me toward the food. I had a very light lunch and I'm famished."

"Of course, anything you like. All you have to do is ask." He took her hand and squeezed it.

The buffet table was loaded with every delicacy anybody could possibly want. Waiters were slicing turkeys, hams and roasts of beef, and silver chafing dishes held pastas and delicate crepes, some filled with chicken, others with lobster. There was also cold seafood displayed on a huge dome of shaved ice, and salads of every variety.

"It all looks so delicious," Suzanna said. "I don't know what to choose."

"Let me bring you a selection." Morgan walked her toward the tables on the lawn.

"You shouldn't wait on me," she protested.

"Why not?"

"I'm not familiar with royal rules of protocol, but I'd bet the farm that kings don't wait on ordinary people."

"I don't see anybody ordinary," he said with a melting smile. "Besides, I want to do it."

Paulette was waving at them from a table nearby where she was sitting alone. "Come sit with us. Marcelle is getting us something to eat."

"Good, I'll join him and be right back," Morgan said.

"I couldn't stand up on these four-inch heels another minute,'' Paulette said. ''I'd like to see the fashion gurus wear a pair for an entire evening.''

''They were undoubtedly designed by men,'' Suzanna said. ''The same guys who design flat, comfortable lace-ups for themselves. Why do we put up with it?''

''For the same reason we buy hundreds of dollars worth of cosmetics—to look good for guys who don't deserve us. But don't tell Estelle I said that.'' Paulette laughed.

They were discussing the new shades of lipstick when Morgan returned, accompanied by a nice-looking man he introduced as Marcelle Dumont. Two waiters were following them, carrying plates loaded with food.

''I selected a little of everything,'' Morgan announced.

Suzanna was sure she couldn't eat that much, but the food was so delicious that she managed to. The company was even more enjoyable. Everybody was so relaxed and friendly that she found it difficult to believe she was actually having dinner with a king!

The conversation eventually turned to horses, and the others discussed a polo match the next day. Suzanna listened with interest, trying to figure out what they were talking about.

Finally Morgan became aware of her silence. ''Don't you care for polo?'' he asked.

''I don't know. I've never seen it played,'' she admitted.

''We'll have to remedy that immediately. Would

you like to come to the match tomorrow? You can cheer me on.''

''I'd love to come, but I won't know if you're winning or losing. Do you have to put the ball through a wicket or in a cage? Something like that?''

He chuckled. ''It's a little different from croquet or hockey. You'll see.''

''We can sit together, and I'll explain it to you,'' Paulette promised.

The rest of the evening seemed to fly by. It was late when they left, but Suzanna didn't want the night to end.

She and Morgan made small talk on the way home, but her mind was only partly on their conversation. She kept wondering if he was finally going to kiss her good-night.

He held her hand going up the grand staircase of the castle, and Suzanna was taut with anticipation. When they reached the landing where the stairs branched off in different directions, Morgan said he would walk her to her door.

''You don't have to,'' she told him, merely being polite. ''It's late, and you have a polo match in the morning.'' She thought he'd brush that aside as inconsequential.

Morgan's calm expression didn't reveal his inner turmoil. Was he relieved or disappointed? he wondered. Suzanna no doubt recognized the risk as well as he did. The sexual attraction between them couldn't be denied, yet neither wanted to get involved—which could easily happen now that they were finally alone. There was also the danger that if he rushed her, she could withdraw from him completely. He had to respect her wishes, but Lord, how he wanted her!

Morgan's emotions weren't visible as he kissed her hand and said, "I'll see you at ten in the morning, then."

"I'm looking forward to it," she answered, concealing her disappointment.

So much for romantic, adolescent dreams, she told herself ironically as they went in different directions. She'd been so sure Morgan would insist on walking her to her room. It served her right for playing silly games. But how could she have read his signals so incorrectly? Obviously she'd overestimated his interest in her.

Morgan didn't act like a disinterested man. At the polo match the next day he came over to where Suzanna was sitting whenever they had a time-out—or whatever they called them. She never quite figured out what was going on.

"It looks quite dangerous," she remarked nervously to Paulette. The players were leaning perilously out of their saddles to whack a ball as other horses thundered straight at them.

"There are occasional injuries, but you don't need to worry about Morgan. He's an expert rider."

Suzanna couldn't help worrying. She was glad when the match was over and a group of them went to a tavern to celebrate. Morgan draped his arm casually around her shoulders as they clustered around the bar, which certainly added to her enjoyment.

He continued to send her mixed messages. There was no doubt about his admiration, and he seemed to enjoy her company, but that was as far as it went.

He took her out with his friends, and she discovered they were almost like her friends at home—except wealthier and more glamorous. But in spite of leading lives of privilege, they worked at meaningful jobs.

Suzanna enjoyed everything she did with Morgan, but especially the times when they were alone. On weekend mornings they often played tennis together, just the two of them. She began to look forward to those games.

But one Saturday morning Morgan phoned to postpone their game because of a diplomatic matter. He suggested she wait in his apartment. Hopefully, they could still play a few sets before lunch.

Their tennis date had been for ten-thirty, but as the time dragged on, it seemed unlikely that they'd get to play. Suzanna sighed and sat on the couch to read the book she'd brought. After a while she took off her tennis shoes and tucked her feet under her. But that got uncomfortable, so she stretched out full-length with pillows under her head.

Suzanna drifted off to sleep and dreamed of Morgan. He was standing across a long room with his back to her. She called out to him, but he didn't hear her. When she tried to raise her voice, he walked out the door.

Suzanna awakened to see Morgan standing over her, looking down at her tenderly.

"It's all right, darling." He smoothed her hair gently. "I won't let anything hurt you."

She opened her eyes and felt happiness flood through her. "You came back!" she exclaimed.

He sat facing her and put his arms loosely around her waist. "I told you I would. I always keep my promises."

"No, you don't understand. I dreamed that you walked away from me without looking back. I knew it was forever. I tried to call to you, but you just kept on going." She threw her arms around his neck and clung so tightly that her breasts were crushed by his hard chest.

Morgan's arms tightened reflexively, and he held her for a long moment. Then his embrace loosened reluctantly. "You're dreaming, Suzanna," he said. "Wake up."

"I am awake," she said softly.

Maybe the dream made her realize how painful it would be to lose Morgan, or maybe she just finally admitted to herself that she was madly and irrevocably in love with him, king or no king. It wasn't sexual attraction or the glamour of his position. It was true, enduring love, the kind that happens only once in a lifetime.

Morgan's body was taut as he examined her face intently. "Are you sure you know what you're doing?"

Suzanna smiled enchantingly. "Why don't you kiss me? I'll bet that would wake me up."

"My darling! You don't know how I've hoped for

this moment." He hugged her so tightly that she could hardly breathe.

Then his mouth closed over hers for a kiss that set them both on fire. His tongue parted her lips and probed the warm recess beyond, staking an unmistakable male claim that was irresistible.

Their hands moved over each other possessively as they reassured themselves that the dream had finally come true. Suzanna traced the width of Morgan's shoulders, then the lean triangle of his torso that rippled now with straining muscles. She pulled his shirt out of his slacks, wanting to feel his warm, bare flesh.

Morgan arched his back when she raked her nails lightly up his spine. "Ahh, darling, I knew it would be like this. It's been driving me crazy not being able to hold you this way."

"I thought you never would." She sighed. "I was almost convinced that you didn't want me."

"You'll never know how much!" He strung a line of kisses down her neck. "This is what I wanted to do every time I looked at you."

His mouth continued its downward, inflaming path over her breast. Suzanna shivered with delight when his teeth nipped gently at her nipple. The feeling was even more erotic, somehow, through the thin cotton of her tennis dress.

Morgan slid the back zipper of her dress down as far as it would go, which was several inches below her waist. He unhooked her bra and smoothed his palms over her bare skin, down to her ruffled bikini panties.

"This is another thing I wanted to do," he murmured as his fingers slipped inside the waistband of her panties.

"Why didn't you?" she asked breathlessly.

"I couldn't take the chance of losing you," he answered, kissing her tenderly. "It had to be what you wanted, too."

"You can't have any more doubts," she said softly as she sat up facing him and slipped the dress off her shoulders.

Morgan's eyes blazed as he gazed at her bare breasts. He cupped them in his palms and leaned down to drop kisses over each firm white mound. Then his lips closed over one nipple and he suckled gently.

Suzanna's passion rose like a warm tide. She linked her arms loosely around Morgan's neck, tilted her head back and closed her eyes to savor the erotic pleasure he was bringing her.

"You're so responsive, angel." He stood and gathered her in his arms. "I want to make you happier than you've ever been."

"I don't think I could be any happier than I am right this minute," she said as he carried her into the bedroom.

"You want to bet?" He smiled sensuously as he placed her tenderly on the bed without letting her out of his embrace.

"That's a bet I'm not going to mind losing," Suzanna said with a seductive glance. She had unbuttoned his shirt, and now she unbuckled his belt.

Morgan stood for a brief moment to shuck off his clothes. Her anticipation mounted as she watched his lithe movements. When he was completely nude, she stared with awe at his splendid physique, dominated now by his rampant manhood.

He returned to straddle her body, with one knee on either side of her hips. Suzanna's heart began to race as he leaned down to kiss her navel while slowly stroking her thighs.

"Your body is so perfect, sweetheart," he said huskily. "I want to know every secret inch of you."

Her passion rose as he removed her dress and panties and gently parted her legs. She gasped when his fingers trailed along her inner thighs to the hot, quivering core of her being that was crying out for him.

"Please, Morgan," she said, moving her legs restlessly.

"Tell me what you want." His eyes were like live coals as he touched her intimately.

"I want you—now!" She pulled him toward her and kissed him frantically.

"Not half as much as I want you," he said with a groan of satisfaction.

With his hands on her hips, Morgan plunged into her, bringing such erotic pleasure that their cries of delight mingled in a joyous duet. Suzanna arched her back to receive all of his driving force, and pursued him when he retreated. Their bodies strained wildly as each wave of sensation mounted higher than the last.

They reached the summit at the same time, holding each other tightly while shock waves pounded through them, then gradually diminished. The downward spiral brought its own kind of pleasure, a mellow warmth that filled them with quiet happiness.

Neither stirred for a long time. They were content just to lie in each other's arms, now that their urgency had been replaced by an inner glow.

Finally Morgan opened his eyes and smiled drowsily at her. "Did I make you happy, sweetheart?"

"Happier than I thought possible," she answered. But she knew it couldn't last.

Right now they were a man and a woman who'd just shared something incredibly beautiful. But once they left this room, Morgan was a king. They had no future together.

Suzanna moved closer to him, refusing to think about anything but this wonderful experience.

They would have weeks together, at the very least. And she was going to enjoy every minute of them, Suzanna vowed.

Chapter Seven

Suzanna and Morgan dozed off in each other's arms after their soul-satisfying lovemaking. She awakened some time later to find him gazing at her with renewed ardor. Even without the light in his eyes, the signs were unmistakable when he moved sensuously against her.

"You're a very vigorous man." She laughed.

"You didn't honestly think I was going to be satisfied that easily?" He stroked her breast lingeringly, arousing her own desire. "I'll never get enough of you, my darling."

They made love again, more leisurely this time, savoring the pleasure they brought each other. Morgan carried out his desire to know every private inch of her. He sought out all the secret places that made her quiver with desire, and Suzanna did the same to him.

When their arousal became too demanding to be delayed, Morgan completed their union. He held her tightly as their bodies moved faster and faster to the wild music that was building to a crescendo. The climax, when it came, left them drained of everything except pleasure.

They were lying spent in each other's arms afterward when the telephone on the bedside table rang. Suzanna started to move away so he could answer it, but Morgan's embrace tightened.

"Let it ring," he growled.

"I'm proud of you," she said, settling back in his arms. "Most people can't bear to let a telephone ring."

"Nothing could be more important than you, so why should I answer it?"

"You won't get an argument from me." She smiled.

"Beautiful girl." He propped himself up on one elbow and kissed her. "Do you know what I'm going to do right now?"

"Again? You're awesome!"

"No, we'll save that for dessert." He chuckled. "First I'm going to order lunch. We didn't have any."

"It's kind of late for that," Suzanna said doubtfully.

"Fortunately I have an in with the chef."

The telephone rang again as soon as he had hung up after giving instructions to the kitchen. Morgan's guarded response told her the caller was a woman. Suzanna got out of bed and gathered up her clothes.

He put his hand over the mouthpiece. ''Where are you going?'' he asked sharply.

''To take a quick shower,'' she answered calmly.

It would be foolish to get upset, Suzanna told herself as she turned on the water. Did she expect his former girlfriends to just disappear now that she and Morgan had made love? At least, she hoped they would be *former* girlfriends. But why worry about that now? At this point in time, Morgan was all hers, and that was what mattered, she thought as she got dressed.

Morgan had ordered lunch served at a small table in the den, rather than the more formal dining room with its long table and stately chairs. They were almost finished eating when his brother stopped by.

''Alicia phoned a short time ago,'' Morgan remarked to his brother. ''I think she was angling for a date to the charity bazaar.''

''Are you going to take her?'' Kenneth asked in a casual voice.

''No, I thought Suzanna might enjoy going, although I haven't gotten around to asking her yet.''

''I'd love to go,'' she said promptly. ''What exactly is it, a dinner dance?''

''Nothing that fancy. It's more like a street fair,'' Morgan explained. ''Every year we take over a big lot on the edge of town and bring in rides for the children and carnival games. You know, knocking down milk bottles to win a prize, that sort of thing. All the money goes to children's charities.''

"Morgan conceived the idea when he took the throne, and it was so popular it became an annual event."

"It sounds like great fun," Suzanna said.

"I think you'll have a good time. I believe the bazaar is quite soon, isn't it?" Morgan looked questioningly at his brother.

"A week from Sunday." Kenneth hesitated, then chose his words carefully. "Perhaps Suzanna would prefer to go with Paulette. I'm sure she's planning to attend."

Morgan's jaw firmed. "I've already asked Suzanna to go with me."

She gave the two men a puzzled look. "Is there some reason why Morgan shouldn't take me? Did you already make another date?" she asked him.

"No, certainly not," he said.

"He won't tell you, but I think you should know," Kenneth said. "Morgan opens the fair every year, and for the first couple of hours, members of the nobility run the booths. It's just a gimmick, but the people like it. They get to talk to duchesses and princes," he said with a self-effacing gesture of his hand. "Morgan's date, if he takes one, should be a royal who works one of the booths."

"It's a silly custom that simply evolved because at the initial fair, everybody I asked to help just happened to have a title. That doesn't mean it's written in stone."

"It's a clever idea and I agree with Kenneth," Suzanna said. "The people are expecting glamour, so I think you should take a princess. Certainly nobody lower in rank.'' She was willing to give up her date for a good cause, but that didn't include handing Morgan over to the boorish Sophia.

His annoyance dissolved into amusement. ''You don't think a countess would suffice?''

''No,'' Suzanna said firmly. ''How about Alicia? She is a princess, isn't she?''

''A very lovely one, but I'm taking you,'' Morgan said. ''Why don't you ask Alicia, Kenneth?''

''I'm not the one she wants to go with.''

Suzanna could see in his eyes the bleakness that Morgan missed. She felt sorry for Kenneth. He was clearly attracted to Alicia, and Morgan didn't seem to have a clue. But it wasn't up to her to interfere, especially between brothers. The matter still wasn't settled when there was a knock at the front door.

Morgan frowned. ''Who could that be? People aren't supposed to disturb me here—with the exception of you, Ken.''

His brother grinned. ''Does that mean you have to put up with me because I'm family?''

''Just go see who's at the door,'' Morgan said affectionately.

Kenneth returned from the entry a few moments later, followed by Rudolph Jablon. The finance minister looked as dour as always. His disapproval deepened when he saw Suzanna sitting at the table with Morgan, then became even more harsh when he noticed her extremely casual attire.

Suzanna had trouble stifling her laughter. If he thought this tennis dress was brief, he should have seen her a little earlier! She glanced at Morgan to share the joke, but his face was set.

"What is it, Jablon?" he asked curtly, which wasn't like him. Morgan was usually so courteous. There always seemed to be tension between the two men, however.

"I'm sorry to bother you, Your Highness. Your secretary said you were in your apartment, so I called earlier, but no one answered." The older man paused, as if waiting for an explanation. When Morgan merely looked at him austerely, he said, "Yes, well, that's why I'm here."

"What is it you want, Jablon?" Morgan asked.

"I think we should discuss your housing project at greater length."

"There's nothing to discuss. The country needs affordable housing, and I intend to build it," Morgan said flatly.

"The council doesn't agree that your plans need to be that extensive. Monrovia is a wealthy country, but our treasury isn't unlimited."

"Most of the money will come from bond issues. There won't be any drain on the treasury."

"Even so," Jablon insisted, "you could cut the cost in half by eliminating the recreation areas and other frills. They are completely unnecessary."

Morgan's face became more forbidding. "Even the disadvantaged are entitled to some quality of life. And while I am king, they will have it."

As the argument promised to escalate, Suzanna murmured, "If you'll excuse me, I think I left something in the living room."

"I'll go with you," Kenneth said.

"No! Both of you stay," Morgan ordered. "Jablon and I are through here."

The older man's mouth was a thin, pinched line as he stared at the king furiously. Morgan's gaze didn't waver, and after a moment Jablon's eyes shifted. "I am sorry to have bothered you, Your Highness."

Kenneth broke the silence after the older man left. "Was that wise, Morgan?" he asked quietly. "Jablon wields a lot of power on the council. He could be a problem."

"He was a problem to Father before I took over the throne! Jablon wants a puppet king he can control, and nothing else will satisfy him. I'm through trying to reason with him. Now I'll do it my way. I am still the reigning monarch."

Suzanna hadn't intended to say anything, but she was burning with curiosity. "If he's so obstructive, couldn't you remove him from the council? You have the last word, don't you?"

"Yes, but the action might be misconstrued. Jablon has served on the council since my grandfather's day. The people don't know that he's a lonely, bitter old man who is living in the past."

"Jablon's wife died years ago, and he never had any children," Kenneth explained. "The council is his whole life. He considers Morgan an intruder in *his* domain."

"All the more reason to get rid of him," Suzanna said.

"I might have to." Morgan sighed. "But I'm trying to avoid it. How can I take away a man's entire reason for living?''

''You're a very nice man,'' she said softly.

Morgan and Suzanna were supposed to go with a group of his friends to a nightclub that night, but by mutual consent, they decided to stay home. Their relationship was so new that they didn't want to share their time with other people.

''I'm sorry if I was selfish,'' Morgan said, stroking her hair lovingly as they lay in each other's arms that night. ''I'll bet you really wanted to go out tonight.''

''You'd lose that bet.'' She curled up closer to him. ''Everything I want is right here.''

''Darling girl.'' His kiss was as sweet as the passion they'd just shared. ''You're very special to me.''

''I hope so,'' she said in a muted voice.

''What can I do to show you how I feel?''

''I shouldn't have said that. You've been wonderful,'' she said remorsefully. Why was she spoiling this beautiful moment? She knew there had been other women, but for this enchanted time, she was the only one who mattered in his life.

''Darling Morgan.'' Suzanna threw her arms around his neck. ''I don't think I could ever be happier than I am right this minute.''

''Let's put that theory to a test,'' he said with a deep male chuckle as he slid her body under his.

No matter how often they made love, each time seemed more wonderful than the last. Morgan aroused her expertly, with whispered words and intimate caresses that made Suzanna twist with rapture in his arms. She thrilled as he searched out every erotic spot guaranteed to give her pleasure.

Then when her body was taut with passion and she was near the edge, he joined their bodies and guided her into their own private world. She clung to him during the turbulence that surged through them again and again before reaching its peak.

Morgan continued to hold her in the calm aftermath.

"It's been quite a momentous day," Suzanna finally said, sighing.

He smiled wickedly. "Wait until you see how I intend to wake you in the morning."

She gave him a startled look. "I can't stay here all night with you."

"Of course you can! Where do you think you're going?"

"Back to my own room."

"Why would you want to do a silly thing like that?" He scissored one leg around both of hers and dipped his head to kiss her breast. "I'll make it much more interesting for you here."

"There's no doubt about that, but I still can't stay."

When Morgan realized she meant it, he gave her a puzzled stare. "What's wrong, Suzanna? I don't know about you, but I thought what we just shared was beautiful. It isn't merely about sex for me. Is that all I mean to *you?*"

She couldn't help laughing. "That's usually what the woman says to the man."

"I'm serious!"

Her laughter faded as she sat up and wrapped the sheet around herself. "You're the most wonderful thing that ever happened to me, Morgan. This whole day with you has been like a fairy tale. Unfortunately we live in the real world. You're a king. Nothing can change that."

"What earthly difference does that make?"

"You're not thinking clearly. If I stayed with you tonight, somebody would be certain to see me leaving in the morning. You know how it would look."

Morgan scowled. "Nobody would dare say anything to you!"

"I'm sure you're right, but the story would spread rapidly. Everybody would know we're having a relationship."

"I didn't think about how this could affect you," Morgan said slowly. "I wouldn't hurt you for anything in the world."

"I'm not worried about myself, darling. I'm thinking of you. People wouldn't approve of your having an affair with someone like me."

"I don't know what people you keep talking about, but it doesn't concern them."

"I wish it were that simple." Suzanna sighed. "Shall I list the strikes against me? To begin with, I'm a commoner. Even worse, I'm an American, which means I don't have any royal blood or even a distant connection to it."

"Every woman I've been interested in hasn't been titled."

"Maybe not, but they were famous in some field, or they came from wealthy families with social standing. I'm not exciting or glamorous. I'm just an ordinary worker.''

''You're the most exciting woman I've ever known.'' Morgan kissed her sweetly. ''But I understand what you're saying, and I would never cause you a moment's embarrassment. There's a very simple solution. I'll have the suite next to mine prepared for you.''

Suzanna laughed helplessly. ''Don't you think everyone would figure it out when you gave me such preferential treatment?''

''I don't give a damn what anyone thinks! We're keeping up appearances—for your sake, not mine,'' he stressed. ''That should be enough.''

She'd seen how adamant Morgan could be when he was opposed head-on, so she tried a light touch. ''There's another reason why it isn't a good idea. It's too far for me to walk to work in the morning,'' she said jokingly.

He looked at her in surprise. ''You don't have to work anymore. I want you here with me.''

Suzanna's eyes narrowed and she stopped trying to placate him. ''I'm not a lapdog, Morgan. I can't sit around waiting for you to come home and pet me, and I can't simply walk out on the job I was hired for.''

''I apologize. I never meant to trivialize your contribution to my country. All of Monrovia is in your debt.''

Suzanna's tense body relaxed. How could she not accept such a handsome apology? She gave him a warm smile. ''Okay, as long as we understand each other.''

''I don't know if I'll ever understand you, but I'm going to try.''

The charity bazaar was well attended, as always. It was a beautiful, balmy Sunday and the people enjoyed this once-a-year opportunity to mingle with royalty, up close and personal.

Suzanna and Kenneth had convinced Morgan that the three of them and Alicia should go to the bazaar in a group, and Suzanna would be a spectator instead of running one of the booths. It solved the problem. Everyone would assume that Morgan was with the princess.

Morgan's booth was the most crowded, naturally. His subjects really doted on their king, with good reason. He had a pleasant or joking word to say to everybody, and he was especially good with the children. He overcame their awe easily, and made sure that each one left with a prize.

Suzanna's heart brimmed with love and pride as she watched him in action. Finally she dragged herself away to wander through the grounds, enjoying the bazaar like everyone else. Until Sophia caught up with her.

''I might have known you'd be here,'' the woman sneered. ''When are you going to stop chasing after Morgan? It's not going to do you any good.''

''I assume you're speaking from experience,'' Suzanna answered sweetly.

Sophia's face flushed unbecomingly. ''You won't

be so smug when Morgan dumps you—like all the rest. He just amuses himself with women like you. When he's ready to settle down he'll choose someone from his own class.'' She walked away without giving Suzanna a chance to reply.

Suzanna kept her head high, refusing to show that the other woman's barbs had hit their target. Sophia might be right about the future, but Suzanna didn't intend to let a petty, vengeful woman spoil the present.

She was enjoying the sunshine and eating pink cotton candy when Alicia came out from behind her ring-toss booth. Relief workers gave the royals a fifteen-minute break every hour. Suzanna had timed it so she could intercept Alicia.

The princess gave her a lukewarm greeting. She'd never been as overtly hostile as Sophia, but she clearly regarded Suzanna as another rival for Morgan's affections.

''Are you making lots of money for charity?'' Suzanna asked.

''Yes, I've been really busy. It's very gratifying.''

''I saw all the young men crowded around. Your booth and Kenneth's are the busiest—except that his customers are all women,'' Suzanna remarked ingenuously.

''You have the wrong Souverain brother. You must mean Morgan.''

''Naturally everybody wants a word with the king, but Kenneth is the one they don't get to see that often. Women are crazy about charming but slightly aloof men. You should see them trying to touch his hand when they give him their money.''

Alicia looked thoughtful. ''I never thought of Kenneth that way.''

''It's probably a good thing. He has all the dates he can handle—as I'm sure you do, too,'' Suzanna added politely.

''Well, yes, but I'm not really involved with anyone right now.''

''Kenneth isn't, either, although I think he's just getting over a failed relationship. That might be why he's dating so many different women. He's afraid of getting hurt again.''

Suzanna realized she was meddling dangerously. Both of the Souverain brothers would be royally displeased if they ever found out. But Suzanna had become friends with Kenneth, and she knew his aloofness was a defense mechanism to cover his shyness. She airily dismissed the prospect of their wrath. Men never knew what was good for them.

''I'm glad you told me,'' Alicia said. ''Kenneth is an old friend. Maybe I can do something to cheer him up. Breakups are so sad. Do you know who he was seeing?''

''No, and you mustn't tell anyone I told you,'' Suzanna said hurriedly. ''He'd be furious with me!''

''I won't say a word,'' Alicia promised. She gave her a speculative look. ''You seem to have gotten very friendly with Kenneth.''

''Only because of my work at the castle. We run across each other frequently, and we often have time to chat while I'm waiting for Morgan to look over some progress reports." Suzanna improvised to explain her frequent visits to Morgan. "Kenneth is fascinating to talk to. He's so knowledgeable about music and the theater."

"I'm interested in those things, too," Alicia said.

"Then maybe you could ask him to join you the next time a group of you are going to a play or a concert. I'm sure he'd appreciate it."

"There's a new play opening next week. I'll ask him to that."

Before Suzanna could reply, Morgan joined them. "Are you getting along all right on your own?" he asked her, after nodding to Alicia.

"I'm having a wonderful time. How is your dart game going? Are you still giving out prizes even if they don't break the balloon?"

He smiled. "Everybody likes to win something."

Alicia wasn't really listening. "Have you seen Kenneth?" she asked suddenly.

"Yes, he's over at the food court getting a soft drink."

"I'll see you both later," she said.

Morgan looked surprised as Alicia hurried off. "That's the first time she's ever done that. What just happened?"

"How spoiled can you get?" Suzanna teased. "You can't believe a woman would willingly leave your side."

"You know that's not what I meant," he protested.

"Well then, maybe Alicia finally figured out there were easier fish to catch and she went to drop her line somewhere else. I guess you're stuck with *me*." Suzanna grinned.

Morgan put his hand under her chin and tilted her face up to his. "It better be the kind of glue that never lets go, because I don't want to lose you."

She felt herself melting at the flame in his eyes. Morgan's passion always sparked her own desire, whether they were alone or in a crowd. She glanced away to lessen the spell—and her eyes met Rudolph Jablon's.

The finance minister was standing a short distance away, staring at them with his customary expression, disapproval. Suzanna started to move back, but Morgan's hand tightened on her chin.

"Hold still." He took a handkerchief out of his pocket. "You have something on your cheek."

"It's probably cotton candy," she mumbled.

"Then I'll just lick it off. I like cotton candy."

"Morgan! Behave yourself. There are people around." She glanced over, but Jablon had left. "I don't know what I'm going to do with you."

"I have a suggestion." He whispered something in her ear that made her blush.

By the time the long, eventful day was over, Morgan and Suzanna were both in a high state of anticipation.

As soon as the door to his apartment was closed, he took her in his arms for a kiss so torrid her legs threatened to buckle.

"I couldn't have waited for this much longer," he

said, gazing into her eyes as he unzipped the back of her dress.

"You deserve a reward for being so patient." She smiled sensuously, removing his tie and unbuttoning his shirt.

Her dress slithered to the floor and he unfastened her bra and tossed that aside, too. "Can I kiss you everywhere?"

"That would be *my* reward," she murmured.

"We'll share it."

He dipped his head and strung a line of kisses over her breasts and down her quivering body to her navel. Then as he rolled her panty hose over her hips, his lips continued along the same path.

Suzanna cried out with joy as Morgan's hot mouth stoked the fire that was already raging in her loins. She clutched at his thick hair to steady herself while he fed her passion.

"My darling girl, I'd do anything for you," he said huskily. "Tell me what you want."

"You, lover, only you," she breathed.

Their coupling was frantic and impassioned. Morgan tore off his clothes and made love to her right there on the plush carpet. They were consumed by their love for each other, both vying to give the most pleasure.

After the storm had passed, he pulled down a pillow from the couch and tucked it under Suzanna's head. Both were too satisfied to say anything, or even to move from the spot.

When her breathing slowed to a steady rhythm,

Morgan smiled fondly. "I'd better get you into bed. You're falling asleep."

Suzanna's eyelashes fluttered open and she yawned. "I'm sorry. It's been a busy day."

"No need to apologize. I never object to going to bed with you." He grinned.

But when he would have gathered her up in his arms, she said, "I have an awful lot of work to do tomorrow. I think I'll go back to my room a little earlier tonight."

"It's barely midnight!" Morgan complained.

"We've been together all day and all night—more or less."

"It's never enough," he declared passionately, giving her a deep, drugging kiss. "I want you next to me in bed, warm and close."

Suzanna put her head on his shoulder, wishing it could be that way all night, every night. "All right," she said. "But just for an hour."

Morgan hugged her tightly for a moment, then he said, "No, I'm being selfish. You do look tired." He stood and went over to pick up her dress. Draping it over her, he said with a wry smile, "But put this on quickly, please. My willpower is notoriously limited where you're concerned."

"I'd worry if it wasn't," she said affectionately.

He took her in his arms and nuzzled her neck.

Finally she pulled away reluctantly. "If I don't leave now, I'll be here all night."

"The welcome mat is always out." When she hesitated, Morgan lifted her arms and pulled the dress over her head. "This is a switch, isn't it?" he joked.

"I'm used to *undressing* you, not the other way around."

"Tomorrow night we'll go back to the old way." With a last, lingering kiss, she left.

Suzanna didn't notice the shadowy figure standing at the end of the hall. She was busy straightening her dress and smoothing her disheveled hair. It spooked her to come upon Jablon so suddenly.

"Oh! I didn't see you there," she exclaimed. "You startled me."

"I could tell you had other things on your mind." He sneered.

Suzanna was determined not to let this disagreeable man upset her. "It's late," she said coolly. "I have to go."

"Not yet." He put his hand on her arm. "I want to talk to you."

She jerked her arm away. "We have nothing to say to each other."

"You're right in one respect. I will do the talking, you will listen. Are you stupid enough to believe nobody knows about your affair with the king?"

"I don't think our relationship is anyone else's business," she answered evenly.

"That's where you're wrong. Everything His Majesty does is my business! I didn't say anything when he took you to bed, even though you were unsuitable. After all, Morgan is a lusty young man." Jablon shrugged. "But it's completely inappropriate for him to be seen with you in public.

"You are a nobody," he said contemptuously. "A commoner without background, a foreigner. What do you expect to get out of the king? Money? I'll give you that if you'll pack up and leave tomorrow.''

Suzanna's blue eyes glittered with anger. ''I don't want anything from Morgan. I wouldn't take anything if he offered it. I enjoy simply being with him.''

''How long do you think you can hold his interest? There have been prettier girls before you and they didn't last.''

''Then you have nothing to worry about, do you?''

His face darkened. ''Your kind of woman can make a man lose all common sense. The way he flaunts you in public is unacceptable. I won't allow it!''

''Then I suggest you talk to Morgan,'' Suzanna said. They both knew how *he* would react. ''We have a saying in my country—It takes two to tango.''

Jablon's eyes narrowed with rage. ''Don't overestimate your power over the king. I am not without my own power. I can destroy both of you if I choose.''

''I think we understand each other, so there's no point in prolonging this conversation.'' She looked him straight in the eye. ''I don't know what you're going to do right now, but I'm going to bed.'' She pushed by him when he didn't get out of her way.

But Suzanna wasn't as calm as she pretended. Back in her own room she paced the floor, reliving the ugly scene. Jablon was only bluffing, she assured herself. He couldn't really hurt Morgan. Hadn't today shown what a popular king he was? The people had always been tolerant of his relationships.

She was the one who was vulnerable, not Morgan.

Suzanna didn't want to be thought of as the king's latest mistress. It would damage her professional reputation and hurt her parents. It would be humiliating for them to read all the innuendos about their daughter and a bachelor king who was considered a playboy. It made her uneasy that two people today had taken great pleasure in predicting that Morgan would tire of her.

Only the remembrance of Morgan's tender lovemaking loosened the tight band around her heart.

Chapter Eight

Jablon called Morgan early the next morning, requesting to see him immediately.

When he arrived, the finance minister got right to the point. "Your relationship with Miss Bentley is completely inappropriate, Morgan," he said bluntly. "It was bad enough when your revered name was linked to models and actresses. I didn't approve, but I remained silent because at least those women were renowned. They even had a certain amount of power—not like yours, of course, but they were influential in their own spheres. With all of that, they were only marginally acceptable. The Bentley woman isn't even in their class!"

"You've decided that?" Morgan asked softly.

"The entire council agrees with me. She's an embarrassment to the throne!"

Morgan's face looked as if it were carved from stone. "How dare you question my choice of companions?"

"Somebody has to tell you your behavior is unseemly. I realize that young men are hot-blooded. Instead of using their brain, they listen to a different part of their anatomy, especially when the girl might be considered desirable."

"I'm surprised you remember what passion is," Morgan drawled. "If you ever indulged in anything so frivolous, that is."

Jablon's thin lips tightened. "You have to get rid of her, Morgan."

"I don't have to do anything of the sort. May I remind you that I am the king of this country?"

"It's for the good of Monrovia that I'm telling you this. Why are you being so stubborn? She's just another girl. You certainly can't marry her. She's a nobody!"

Morgan's jaw set as he stood and towered regally over the other man. "You will show more respect when speaking of Miss Bentley—and you will refer to her by name, not as that girl or that woman."

"I might have known she'd complain to you," Jablon muttered.

"What did you say to her?" Morgan asked sharply.

"I merely pointed out all the things I've told you. That she was jeopardizing your position by this reckless affair. The people would disapprove strongly. If this girl—Miss Bentley," Jablon corrected himself, stressing the name sarcastically. "If she really cares for you, as you think, she'll go back where she belongs and put an end to this nonsense.''

"If anyone leaves it will be you, Jablon!" Morgan thundered. "You've been quarrelsome and obstructive for as long as I've known you, but this time you've gone too far."

"I'm simply doing my duty to my country," the man said stubbornly.

"Are you implying that I'm not?" Morgan asked ominously.

Instead of answering the question, Jablon said, "Can't you see what that woman is doing? She's driven a wedge between us. You won't listen to me— *me,* your senior, most trusted adviser!"

"That's your description, not mine," Morgan said coldly. "You might have been effective in my grandfather's day, but you've become intolerant and out of touch. Perhaps it's time you retired, Jablon."

"You can't turn me out like a stable boy! I've given my life to the monarchy."

"All of the kings in our long history did the same thing, but they also managed to have a personal life. That's something I intend to have, as well. And don't tell me I can't remove you from your position. You and the entire council serve at my pleasure. If you or any of your colleagues find the situation untenable, I will accept your resignations."

"You don't mean that, Morgan!"

"This audience is at an end," Morgan said regally. "Except for one thing. I don't want to find out you've harassed Miss Bentley again. To do so would be to seriously incur my displeasure. Is that quite clear?"

"Yes, Your Highness," Jablon muttered.

After the finance minister had left, Morgan strode to the door and almost collided with his secretary.

"Your first appointment is here, Your Highness," the man said.

"Tell him to wait. I'll be right back."

Suzanna looked up in surprise when Morgan appeared in her studio. "What are you doing here at this hour? Did you want to make sure I wasn't goofing off?" She grinned.

"Why didn't you tell me Jablon spoke to you?" he asked without preamble.

Her smile faded. "How did you know?"

"That's not important. I want to know why you didn't tell me?"

"I haven't had a chance. He was in the hallway when I left your apartment last night. Do you think he was spying on us, Morgan?"

"I wouldn't put it past him," he answered with a grim face. "What did he say to you?"

"He was slightly unpleasant, but it didn't bother me," she lied. "I know he doesn't like me."

"Tell me what he said."

"He doesn't believe we should be seen in public. I don't think we need to be that secretive, but maybe we should try not to appear so... friendly. Like yesterday at the charity bazaar."

Morgan couldn't help smiling. "I'd say I was pretty restrained, considering what I felt like doing."

"You made up for it later."

He cupped her cheek in his palm and asked softly, "Any regrets?"

"Not a one."

They were gazing into each other's eyes when Brian appeared in the doorway. "Suzanna, we need to—oh, sorry!" He disappeared before she could say anything.

"You see what I mean?" She sighed. "We simply have to be more discreet. I don't want our relationship to create problems for you."

"Let me worry about that."

She looked at him doubtfully. "You told me Jablon is head of the council. That must be an important position. I'm afraid he could make trouble for you."

Morgan's eyes narrowed. "Not nearly as much trouble as I can make for him. I don't think he'll bother you again, but if he does, I want to know about it. Okay?"

"Okay." Suzanna's heart sang as she gazed at the man she loved. Morgan was an omnipotent presence, so confident and capable. Surely a lesser man like Jablon was no threat.

Morgan's jaw was set grimly when Kenneth came to his office a short time later. Jablon's disapproval had only solidified Morgan's desire to keep seeing Suzanna. But the problems still existed. He finally discussed them with his brother.

"I'll back you all the way," Kenneth said. "But you realize the objections Jablon will continue to raise because Suzanna has no title, celebrity status or money. The council will also raise a furor after Jablon gets through stirring them up."

"I couldn't care less," Morgan said dismissively. "I believe the people will back my choice."

"Then why are you talking to me instead of her? Why haven't you proposed?"

Morgan hesitated. "There was an instant flame between Suzanna and me the moment we met. At first I thought it was just sexual attraction. As my feelings for her deepened, I wondered how important my wealth and position were to her. She wouldn't be the first woman who was dazzled by the glamour surrounding a king."

"Suzanna isn't like that," Kenneth protested.

"Still, if it really is love, she couldn't begin to imagine how restricted her life would be as queen of Monrovia. The endless charity functions she'd have to attend, the speeches in front of strangers, the constant scrutiny by the public and press. Would she start to feel harassed from every side, peered at like a bug under a microscope? She's so wonderfully natural. How could I take away her freedom—or see her love for me wither under the strain?"

"That's something you have to talk about together at the time. Then let *her* decide."

"I'll think about doing what you suggest, but everything is so perfect between us now." Morgan's somber expression lightened. "There really isn't any great hurry. I couldn't get married anyway until the year of mourning is up."

Morgan had a busy social life and a multitude of friends. But when he wanted to relax, he shared his leisure hours with a small group of intimates.

Paulette was part of the group, as well as Theo, the man Suzanna had danced with the night Sophia had spirited Morgan away. Unfortunately Sophia was included in the group, as well. Suzanna was less than delighted, but she didn't mention it to Morgan.

The others accepted their relationship without comment or criticism. All except Sophia, who continued to be unpleasant, although she was smart enough to hide her feelings when Morgan was around.

His favorite way to relax was a Sunday-afternoon barbecue around the swimming pool. It wasn't anything like the casual ones Suzanna was used to at home. Servants offered drinks and hors d'oeuvres to the guests lounging on chaises in their bathing suits. Then a chef grilled steaks and chicken in a large brick barbecue.

When it got too cool to swim, the guests changed into informal clothes in the cabanas and the party continued. Some people danced on the terrace to music from the stereo system, others went into the den to watch the latest movies Morgan had ordered.

Suzanna and Morgan often just lounged on chaises next to each other holding hands, content simply to be together.

One typical Sunday evening Morgan watched his brother dancing on the terrace with Alicia. "The advice you gave Kenneth seems to have worked," he commented. "She won't let him out of his sight."

Thanks to Suzanna, Kenneth's relationship with Alicia was thriving. He often asked her for advice, and she subtly steered him in the right direction.

Suzanna smiled. "Sometimes you have to play

games to make the other person jealous so you'll get what you want.''

Morgan turned his head to look at her. ''Are you speaking from experience?''

''I didn't have to play any tricks on you. You wouldn't leave me alone,'' she teased.

''I'm beginning to think I chased you until you caught me,'' he said dryly.

''You aren't permanently trapped. There's nothing to stop you from moving on.'' She kept her voice purposely light, even though just the thought of losing Morgan was agonizing.

''There's only one place I want to go,'' he answered deeply, gazing into her eyes. ''Why don't we say good-night and let the rest of them party on as long as they like?''

''It's only nine o'clock,'' Suzanna said with a bubbly laugh.

Another couple came over to join them before he could answer.

A little later, when Suzanna was alone for a few moments, Sophia came over to her. Morgan had gone into the den to speak to the servants about something.

''I guess you're sorry now that you were so brazen about your affair with Morgan,'' the redhead drawled.

''You're the only one who seems to mind,'' Suzanna answered sweetly.

''Is that what you think?'' Sophia gave her a shark-like smile. ''From what I hear, the natives are getting restless. They don't think you're a proper playmate for their king.''

''That's their opinion, or yours?''

"We both know what *I* think of you." Sophia laughed merrily. "I'm just too much of a lady to use those words."

"You would use anything you could to get rid of me. But it isn't going to work."

"Maybe I can't bring Morgan to his senses, but his council can. I have it on good authority that they're furious at him for sneaking you into his bedroom at night—considering that you're little more than a servant around here."

Suzanna let the insult go by because she was so shocked that Sophia seemed to know about the incident with Jablon. She tried to keep her dismay from showing. "How would you know what Morgan's council thinks?" she asked calmly.

"Do you really believe nobody knows that you and Morgan are sleeping together? There aren't any secrets in the castle."

That's what Suzanna had told Morgan, but she'd thought they'd been discreet. She just hadn't reckoned on somebody actually spying on them.

"If you were any more than a warm body to Morgan, he'd let you stay all night," Sophia taunted.

"I doubt if our sleeping arrangements are of interest to the council. Or to Morgan's subjects, either, for that matter."

"Don't be so sure. If you turn into a full-blown embarrassment it could damage Morgan's popularity. The bad publicity would snowball, and he might even be forced to give up his crown. He has a brother who could take over the throne, you know."

"That's absurd!" Suzanna exclaimed.

"Is it? Think about it. Other royals have been forced to abdicate. Where would that leave you? Nobody would want anything to do with you. You'd be the mistress who brought down a king. Even Morgan would come to hate you."

The two women were so intent that they didn't see Morgan until he was right next to them.

"You ladies look very serious," he said easily, although his eyes were watchful. "What are you talking about?"

"I was telling Suzanna how much I admired the dress she wore to Marie's party," Sophia said smoothly. She glanced away and waved to someone in the distance. "Oh, there's Theo. I just remembered something I have to tell him."

As she hurried off, Morgan said, "You didn't look as if you were discussing clothes."

Suzanna managed a smile. "It's hard to talk to Sophia about anything else."

She had decided against telling Morgan about the gossip that was circulating. He would be furious and would almost surely overreact—which wouldn't solve anything. It was reprehensible of Jablon to have leaked the story, but fires die out if no fuel is added, she reasoned.

Suzanna tried to put the whole ugly matter out of her mind, but Morgan could tell something had upset her. When he tried unsuccessfully to find out what it was, the obvious answer was Sophia. Suzanna let him think that, because it was better than the truth—which would upset *him.*

Their lovemaking when they went to bed that night

was more intense and satisfying than ever. In his attempt to assure her that she meant something to him, Morgan's hands and mouth brought Suzanna to a fevered pitch before fulfilling her completely.

She aroused him in the same way, delighting in the pleasure she could bring him. It was a poignant experience, because pushed to the back of her mind was the knowledge that forces were working against them.

But before the night was over, nestled in Morgan's arms, she felt her fears fade. Sometime in the future they'd have to face up to reality—but not yet.

The storm clouds on the horizon grew closer the next morning. Suzanna was reinforcing the back of a damaged canvas when Brian came into her studio.

"I can see you're busy," he said hesitantly. "But when you have a minute I'd like to talk to you."

"It's okay, I can use a break." She put down the tools and flexed her shoulder muscles. "What's up?"

"I wouldn't mention this if we weren't friends. I mean, it's none of my business, but I heard something I think you should know."

A little chill traveled up Suzanna's spine, but she looked at him calmly. "It sounds serious."

"I guess it could be. That's up to you to decide."

"Are you going to tell me, or just leave me twisting in the wind?" she asked sharply.

"It's about you and the king," he said reluctantly. "A bunch of us went out to some of the clubs over the weekend. We didn't ask you to join us because we know you spend all your spare time with him.

Which is great," Brian said hurriedly. "I don't blame you."

Suzanna had realized long ago that her co-workers were aware of her involvement with Morgan. It was unavoidable, since he was in her studio so often, and she never accepted invitations to join in their activities on the weekends. It was a subject that was tacitly avoided, however.

"Anyway, we heard a bunch of the natives talking in a bar last night. Actually they were having a rather loud argument." He slanted a glance at her. "It was about you and King Morgan. I almost belted one of the guys."

"What did he say?"

"Well, you have to realize they were all kind of drunk. The gist of it was that you weren't good enough for the king. It seems there's a rumor that King Morgan is getting serious about you." Brian looked at her quizzically. When she didn't answer, he continued, "Some of the Monrovians said, so what? The king is entitled to a personal life. But the other guys said he shouldn't be involved with a commoner. They said he should stick to his own kind, or at least women with royal connections. Can you believe these people? In this day and age!"

Suzanna had hoped that Sophia invented that part of her story. It would be like her to make a bad situation worse. But she didn't have to; Jablon had done it for her.

"As I said, your relationship with the king is none of my business—or anyone else's," Brian added. "I just thought you should know what's going around."

"Thanks, Brian, I'm glad you told me."

"Yeah, well, if there's anything I can do—like beat some respect into one of those dudes." He grinned. "Just say the word."

Her shoulders drooped after he left. The idyll had ended sooner than expected. Their relationship was becoming dangerous for Morgan, but she knew he'd be unwilling to give her up. She'd have to be the one to end it. She loved him too much to be the weapon of his destruction.

Very carefully Suzanna put her brushes in a jar of solvent before dialing his extension and asking to see him immediately.

"This is an unexpected pleasure, darling," Morgan said when she appeared in his office a few minutes later. "What's the occasion?"

With as little emotion as possible, Suzanna told him what Brian had relayed to her. She finished by saying, "This means that I'll have to leave Monrovia, of course."

Morgan had listened to the gossip with growing fury; now his expression changed. "You're not going anywhere," he stated firmly.

"You aren't being realistic. If I leave now, the rumors will die out. Next week nobody will remember them. But if I stay, this thing might gain momentum. People are already talking and taking sides."

"People always gossip about royals," he said dismissively. "It's more fun than talking about the weather. I'm sorry that you were subjected to this unpleasantness." His voice softened as he cupped her cheek in his palm. "I want to bring you joy, not cause you pain. You're not to worry about a thing, do you understand? I'll take care of everything.''

Suzanna let herself believe he could do it. Morgan inspired such confidence. This must be one of the reasons his subjects loved him so much, she thought. He was a man of courage. Surely they wouldn't turn against him for a very human frailty.

Suzanna and Morgan avoided the subject by unspoken agreement after that. She was sure he'd read the riot act to Jablon, but he hadn't booted him off the council, she was glad to see. It would only have added grist to the rumor mill, which Morgan must have realized.

Jablon might pride himself on his Machiavellian tactics, but he'd met his match in the king. Suzanna had a feeling there would be a new finance minister when the time was right.

Suddenly she and Morgan had happier things to think about. Kenneth asked them to come to his apartment for cocktails one night. This was a little unusual, because they normally met at Morgan's apartment. He was the sun they all revolved around.

"Why do you think Kenneth wanted us to come to his place?" Suzanna asked as they strolled down a long corridor.

"He probably bought a new painting, or an antique music box he wants to show us. Although it's hard to tell when he'd have time to visit the galleries." Morgan grinned. "He and Alicia are like Siamese twins these days."

Sure enough, the princess was sitting on a couch

when a servant ushered them into the living room. After a few minutes of small talk and when they all had a drink, Kenneth raised his glass.

"I want to propose a toast to the most wonderful girl in the world."

"That's open to interpretation." Morgan smiled and squeezed Suzanna's hand.

"This one promised to be my wife," Kenneth said, exchanging a look of adoration with Alicia.

"Oh, Kenneth, that's wonderful!" Suzanna rushed over and threw her arms around him impulsively.

Morgan followed and clapped his brother on the shoulder. "This is great news! I couldn't be happier for you."

"Isn't anybody going to congratulate the bride-to-be?" Alicia asked plaintively.

Morgan went over and clasped her hands in his while he kissed her on both cheeks. "Kenneth is a lucky man. It's a pleasure to welcome you into the family, my dear."

"This is so exciting," Suzanna said. "I hope I'm invited. I've never been to a royal wedding."

"We couldn't have it without you," Kenneth said fondly. "You're largely responsible."

"You two are perfect for each other," she said. "I'm sure you would have recognized that without my help."

Alicia looked at her curiously. "You knew Kenneth and I were in love before we did?"

"I suspected as much," Suzanna said innocently.

"I can't imagine how." Alicia smiled mischievously at Morgan. "Actually I had a crush on his brother."

"You made the right choice," Morgan said. "They don't come any better than Kenneth."

Suzanna was glad the subject had come up, and been laid to rest so easily. "Have you talked about when you plan to get married?"

"It can't take place for at least four months," Kenneth said. "The year of mourning for Grandmother won't be over until the end of November."

"It will take at least that long to plan the wedding," Alicia said. "There's so much to do—making out the guest list, ordering the invitations, deciding on the floral decorations. And that's only the beginning. There are all the social events and the public celebrations for the townspeople."

"Selecting your wedding gown will be a big project, too," Suzanna said. "It should be something smashing."

"Yes, that's a definite priority," Alicia agreed. "I'll get sketches from some of the top designers. The real problem will be choosing my attendants. You can't have everybody, and there are always hurt feelings."

"It's too bad you don't have the option of eloping," Morgan remarked wryly.

"You don't feel that way, do you, Kenneth?" Alicia pouted.

"I'd go through anything to marry you," he answered dotingly.

"Spoken like a man in love—and a diplomat." Morgan chuckled.

"Now I know why you never married," Suzanna said lightly. "You don't want to go through all the fuss and pageantry."

"He won't mind when his time comes," Alicia said.

"You make it sound so ominous," Morgan joked.

Suzanna felt a stab of pain at his derisive tone. She thought Kenneth's engagement was romantic, but it didn't make Morgan the slightest bit regretful. He didn't want to marry her or anyone else.

"We can announce our engagement, can't we?" Alicia asked.

"Just as soon as possible," Kenneth assured her.

Suzanna put aside her own hurt as the two women discussed the upcoming nuptials. It was exciting to hear all the details involved in a royal wedding—even if she might not be here to see it.

Morgan and his brother gradually moved away and started to talk about other matters.

When Suzanna and Morgan left some time later, she was a little cool toward him, but he didn't seem to notice.

Putting his arm around her shoulders as they walked down the hall, he said, "They both seem really happy, don't they?"

"Yes, I couldn't be more delighted for them."

"I suppose so, since they owe it all to you. You're quite a little matchmaker," Morgan teased.

"I just thought it was time one of the de Souverain men got married," she answered carelessly.

Chapter Nine

The news of Prince Kenneth's engagement to Princess Alicia was greeted with great joy by the people of Monrovia. The young couple were as ecstatically happy as Suzanna and Morgan.

But the storm clouds that seemed to have disappeared now gathered again, more foreboding than before. The first hint of trouble started at a meeting Morgan had with Jablon, after the minister congratulated him on his brother's approaching marriage.

"The people would be even happier if you were the bridegroom," Jablon said artlessly. "They expect you to marry and produce an heir."

"I'm aware of my responsibilities," Morgan said curtly.

"Then fulfill them! Your affair with Miss Bentley has gone on long enough."

Morgan knew a showdown was imminent. "My private life is not subject for discussion," he stated flatly.

"Are you so besotted with the woman that you're willing to give up your crown for her?" Jablon demanded. "Because sooner or later you will have to make a choice."

Morgan's eyes narrowed. "Are you giving me an ultimatum?"

"I'm telling you what is going to happen. If you're unwilling to put the welfare of the country above your own desires, then perhaps you should consider abdicating in favor of your brother. He is marrying someone of his own station. His child will be a proper heir to the throne."

"Don't threaten me, Jablon. I love my country more than you ever could."

"Then do the right thing—or face the consequences."

Morgan drew himself up to his full height and stared expressionlessly at the other man. "You're playing a dangerous game, Jablon. I think you forget which one of us has the power." Without waiting for a reply, he strode out of the room.

Morgan didn't tell Suzanna about his clash with Jablon. The first sign of the gathering storm passed by her almost unnoticed. A little squib in the newspaper mentioned that it should be the king who was getting married instead of his younger brother. That was a valid observation, however, since everyone had been speculating for years on who and when he would marry.

But then a gossip column in one of the more irresponsible newspapers renewed the rumors about Morgan and Suzanna. They suggested it was time he put loyalty above lust—although they didn't use those exact words.

A couple of the letters to the editor were almost that blunt. They said the king should either give up his mistress or devote all his time to her and let his brother run the country.

Suzanna had been concerned; now she was aghast. "This is terrible! We'll have to stop seeing each other immediately."

"We'll do nothing of the sort!" Morgan's eyes glittered with rage as he tossed the newspaper aside.

"Be reasonable, Morgan. If your people are starting to speak out against our relationship, we have to listen."

"Those letters were planted by Jablon. I didn't think he'd go this far, but it seems I underestimated him."

"I know you two clash regularly, but the country is stable under your rule. Why would he create a crisis by forcing you off the throne?"

"For power. He's always resented me for being my own man. He thinks he can manipulate Kenneth more easily. Jablon wants to be the real power behind a talking head."

"Would he actually go that far?" Suzanna asked doubtfully.

"Obviously. But he won't get away with it."

"He's succeeded in stirring things up again. Maybe it would be better if I went home for a while. I can

come back later when things calm down and everybody is too occupied with Kenneth and Alicia's wedding to care about us."

Morgan took her hands and gazed deeply into her
eyes. "Just trust me." He took her in his arms, and
that was the end of the conversation.

Suzanna couldn't see any way out of their dilemma. She knew the wisest thing for both of them
would be for her to leave, but she couldn't bring herself to make the break.

Their lovemaking was frequent and wildly passionate, since both knew their relationship was threatened—even though Morgan refused to admit it. She
tried to pretend along with him, but she was in a
constant state of turmoil.

Soon Suzanna had something even more worrisome
to cope with. Her period was long overdue. She'd
been so distracted that she hadn't kept track.

As the days passed Suzanna grew more tense. She
wasn't sleeping well and she felt like bursting into
tears at the slightest mishap. By the end of the month
she had to face the fact that she was pregnant. Suzanna knew what she had to do.

She waited until after they'd made love. Surely she
was entitled to one last night. Then when they were
both sated in each other's arms, she told him she was
leaving.

"We've been through all this," he said fondly, but
impatiently. "Let's talk about a wedding present for
Kenneth and Alicia. Do you have any idea what
they'd like?"

"I'm serious, Morgan." She drew away and sat up against the headboard. "It isn't only for your sake. I've been gone a long time, and I'm getting homesick."

He sat up as well and looked at her uncertainly. "You never mentioned it before."

"I knew you'd try to talk me out of going, so I put off telling you."

"It was selfish of me not to realize how isolated you must feel here," he said remorsefully. "I've been so happy that I never considered *your* feelings."

"Don't say that. You've been wonderful to me," she said softly. "This has been the best time of my life."

Morgan turned on the bedside lamp so he could examine her face closely. "You don't plan on coming back, do you?"

"I certainly hope to," she said brightly. "But in the meantime we can write to each other and stay in touch by phone." Hopefully he wouldn't call after the first couple of weeks.

"Why won't you trust me to work things out?" he asked gently. "You don't have to run away."

"I'm not leaving because of the gossip. Kenneth is a dear, but I don't think the people would choose him over you just because you had an affair with a commoner."

"Why else would you leave? I'm sure you miss your parents, but I don't believe you suddenly got homesick overnight."

It didn't sound very credible, but what other excuse could she give? "Okay, I lied. I do mind what people are saying about me. I'm not as sophisticated as your glamorous friends. I want to leave before the tabloids splash the story all over the world and everyone at home finds out.''

''Jablon is at the bottom of this,'' Morgan said grimly. ''He started it, and he can stop it—if he knows what's good for him. Give me a week or so, and it will all be over.''

''No!'' Suzanna didn't think she could take much more. ''I'm doing what's best for both of us. Just take my word for it and let me go.''

''There's more to this than you're telling me.'' Morgan grasped her shoulders and forced her to look at him. ''What's in back of your sudden decision? Did Jablon threaten you? If he did, I'll tear him apart with my bare hands!''

''It has nothing to do with him.''

Morgan didn't believe her. He kept pelting her with questions until she felt like a small, trapped animal. Finally her tight control slipped and she shouted at him.

''I'm pregnant! Now do you understand?''

His hands fell away and he gave her a startled look. ''How can that be? I thought you said you were taking…''

''I was. I am. But no birth control is one-hundred-percent effective. Sometimes this just happens.'' When he continued to stare at her, she said, ''You don't have to worry. No one will ever know you're the father.''

''That's a rotten thing to say! What kind of man do you think I am?'' he demanded.

"A very dear one," she said in a softened tone. It eased the tight band around her chest to know he was concerned for her. "But this would give Jablon all the ammunition he needs to get rid of you. An affair can be condoned, but not an illegitimate child."

"Our child will not be illegitimate. We'll get married."

It was what she wanted more than anything. But not this way, not when Morgan was forced into it. "I don't expect you to marry me. I can take care of my own baby."

His expression changed as he looked at her. The shock had worn off. It was replaced by growing excitement. "*Our* baby, angel! Do you know what this means?"

"Yes, it means you could be forced to abdicate," she answered dully.

"Never! Not even if we weren't married. But we will be. Our baby will have its rightful name."

"You're dreaming, Morgan. Even if just possibly your subjects might accept me as their queen, we couldn't marry for at least four months. By that time I'll be visibly pregnant. There's a limit to what you can ask people to overlook."

"I see your point." He looked thoughtful. Then his face cleared. "We'll be married in a small private ceremony. The year-long moratorium was on all *public* celebrations."

"How can you justify not waiting until the year is up?" she asked doubtfully. "It's only four months. Besides, your people have been waiting for years to see you get married. They expect all the pomp and ceremony that goes with a royal wedding. They might feel cheated.''

''Possibly, under ordinary circumstances. But you're forgetting that Kenneth is getting married. The people will have all the spectacle and excitement they want and deserve. This actually ties up all the ends rather neatly. We could scarcely ask Kenneth and Alicia to put off their own marriage so ours could take precedence. But two gigantic weddings in tandem would be overkill.''

Happiness was starting to bubble up inside Suzanna, crowding out all the despair. ''So we're really doing everybody a favor, is that what you're saying?'' She smiled enchantingly.

''Exactly!'' He gathered her close and kissed her. ''I told you to trust me, darling. I knew there had to be a solution to our problems.''

It occurred to Suzanna fleetingly that Morgan had turned a liability into an asset. Once he was married and it was announced after a discreet amount of time that an heir was on the way, Jablon wouldn't be able to budge Morgan off the throne with a crowbar. But she dismissed such suspicions as unworthy. Morgan seemed as thrilled as she was.

Everything happened exactly as Morgan had predicted. His subjects were so charmed by the romance of their king's love affair that they were predisposed to like Suzanna. Especially after they saw her.

Morgan did an end run around Jablon and broke the news of his impending marriage on a television broadcast to the entire nation, with Suzanna standing beside him looking cool and regal. What nobody could tell was that she was numb with terror. So much was riding on his subjects' approval.

She need not have worried, as phone calls of congratulations quickly jammed the castle switchboard and fax machines. More of the same were relayed from newspaper offices. Almost overnight, young girls started wearing their hair long and loose like hers, and costume jewelry stores began advertising copies of Suzanna's magnificent engagement ring. Morgan had given her a gorgeous square-cut diamond set with baguette sapphires on the sides.

In the weeks following their announcement, Alicia explained protocol to her, and the do's and don'ts of royal life. She also took her shopping for a trousseau. That was how Suzanna discovered Morgan's secret arrangement with Gaultiere's. She was appalled at the true prices, and scolded him for the deception. But he just laughed.

And Morgan had made up for lost time by showering Suzanna with presents. Every time they went out—which was often, because there were so many parties given for them—he would present her with another gift of jewelry, a diamond bracelet with matching earrings, a gorgeous sapphire brooch.

The night before the wedding, Suzanna and Morgan had a romantic candlelight dinner in his apartment, just the two of them.

"Sometimes I think I'll wake up back in New York and find this has all been a dream," she said.

"We've never talked about how your life will

change,'' Morgan said slowly. "Are you subconsciously regretting your decision?''

"I didn't have much choice, did I?'' She grinned impishly. "Besides, what woman would object to becoming a queen?''

"I hope it will live up to your expectations.'' The flickering candlelight made his expression unreadable.

"It already has,'' she said fondly. "You've always treated me like a queen. I have something I hope will make *you* happy. It's a wedding present. May I give it to you now? Tomorrow is going to be so hectic we probably won't have any time alone. Not that my gift is anything that special.'' She laughed self-consciously. "You already have everything. This is just a little something I thought you'd like.''

He smiled indulgently. "Now you've really aroused my curiosity. Whatever it is, I'm sure I'll love it.''

Rather diffidently she gave him a small painting she'd done of herself. She'd copied her image faithfully without glamorizing herself the way portrait artists did. The result had surprised even her. It was a picture of a woman in love. Memory had guided her brush, capturing the magic of the night in the gazebo, the way her eyes had sparkled, the love she'd felt for Morgan before she even knew that's what it was.

He was choked with emotion as he gazed at her exquisite face. "This is the most precious thing you could have given me.''

"I hoped it would express my feelings a little more tangibly than words,'' she said softly as he kissed her.

Finally he drew away and said, "My wedding present to you will be an anticlimax.'' He drew a square blue velvet box out of his breast pocket and handed it to her.

Suzanna's eyes widened when she opened the box. Inside on a bed of white satin was a double circlet of diamonds separated by square-cut sapphires and marquise diamonds. Each separate stone blazed like a bright star.

''It's the most gorgeous necklace I've ever seen!'' she gasped. ''I won't ever want to take it off.''

''It's all right with me, as long as that's all you wear to bed tomorrow night,'' he teased.

Suzanna's wedding was everything she'd ever dreamed of. The ceremony was held in the garden in the late afternoon. The guests sat in rows on little gold chairs on either side of a royal blue carpet that stretched from the terrace to the gazebo where the ceremony would take place. Sunlight shone on the roses intertwined in the white latticework, and bird songs mixed with the soft strains of violins played by musicians on the terrace.

Alicia helped Suzanna into her wedding gown. The oval neckline of the sleeveless, cream-colored satin bodice was edged in antique lace, and the full skirt had panels of the same lace. Her veil flowed from a circlet of orange blossoms and stephanotis that were repeated in her bridal bouquet, along with white orchids and lilies of the valley.

''There, that's perfect. You look gorgeous.'' Alicia adjusted the veil another fraction of an inch, then turned toward the door. "I'll go tell everybody you're ready."

Suzanna's feelings were bittersweet as she walked down the hall alone. This was supposed to be the happiest day of her life, but none of her family was there to share it. She'd counted on having her parents there. They'd talked to each other on the phone at least once a week since she'd been in Monrovia, and even oftener after she became engaged. They'd been very excited about coming to the wedding. Then at the last minute her father had come down with an inner ear infection and the doctor said he couldn't get on a plane.

Morgan knew how disappointed Suzanna was. He'd even offered to postpone the wedding, but she'd told him that wasn't practical.

When she stepped through the door, Morgan and Kenneth appeared on either side of her and Alicia preceded them down the plush carpet. As they all walked with a measured beat, both men smiled at Suzanna's startled expression. This wasn't the way they'd rehearsed it!

"We wanted you to know your family is here with you," Morgan murmured.

Tears misted her eyes at their thoughtful concern. What made her think she was alone? These wonderful people had given her a warm feeling of belonging.

The ceremony was very moving. At the conclusion, when Morgan placed the diamond wedding ring on her finger, Suzanna realized she had everything any woman could possibly hope for.

The wedding reception afterward was very festive.

Suzanna met so many royal relatives that she couldn't keep track. Possibly because of the long cocktail hour, followed by dinner with many champagne toasts.

When the evening was finally over and she and Morgan went upstairs, Suzanna was still on cloud nine.

"I know everyone thinks their wedding is perfect, but ours really was." She told Morgan about that moment when she felt she truly belonged.

"We're a family now," he said fondly.

"I know. It means a lot to have Kenneth and Alicia accept me so warmly."

"I was speaking of you and me—and the baby."

She gave him a surprised look. "Would you believe I'd forgotten about it?" Suzanna was so excited she didn't notice the change in Morgan's expression. "We've never discussed it, but I suppose you want a boy, don't you?"

"Not necessarily." He moved away, untying his tie.

"I hope it's a boy for your sake, but in a way, I'd prefer a girl. Then we can keep trying for a boy." She sighed happily. "I'd like to fill up the castle with babies!"

Morgan's reserve vanished and he came back to take her in his arms. "Every time I start to think you can't be this wonderful, you always prove I'm wrong."

Suzanna didn't have time to wonder what Morgan meant, because he cupped her chin in his palm and lifted her face for a tender kiss. Without relinquishing her mouth he unzipped the back of her gown and steadied her while she stepped out of it. All she had underneath was a pair of sheer panty hose.

Morgan held her at arm's length and gazed at her with glowing eyes. "You're so exquisite. I could look at you for hours."

She shrugged his jacket off his shoulders and unbuttoned his shirt. "I can think of a more rewarding activity," she murmured.

"I'm open to suggestions."

He let her undress him because he could tell she wanted to. Suzanna took her time, running her palms over his lean chest, then tracing the triangle of his torso down to his waist.

After unzipping his trousers, she slid her hands inside his briefs and dug her fingers into his taut buttocks. When his clothes were removed and kicked aside, the proof of his passion was impressively evident.

Morgan arched his back when she caressed his rampant manhood. "How is it possible to want anyone this much?" he groaned.

She continued to stroke him sensuously. "Show me how much, darling."

Morgan swung her into his arms and carried her to the bed. Kneeling over her, he rolled down her panty hose, pausing to kiss each inch of bare skin as it was revealed. When he reached her thighs and parted her legs, Suzanna gasped with pleasure.

His mouth lit tiny sparks of excitement that quickly roared into a bonfire. As she twisted and moaned with rapture, his tongue started an earthquake that began to build. When it was about to erupt he plunged inside her, adding his driving force to the molten sensation.

They were completely spent afterward. It was a long time later that Suzanna laughed softly and said, "I'm very glad I don't have to go back to my room tonight."

Morgan's arms tightened. "The best thing about our marriage will be waking up tomorrow with you in my arms."

She looked up at him impishly. "The best thing?"

"Well, one of the good ones, anyway."

They left on their honeymoon aboard the royal yacht the next day. Suzanna couldn't believe the luxury of the ship or the size of the crew, all for just the two of them. She was also startled the first time one of the crew members addressed her as Your Highness.

"I looked around to see if you were behind me," she told Morgan.

"You'll get used to it."

"I guess it feels strange because everything happened so fast."

"Lucky for you. You got to be queen the easy way," he said, pretending to grumble. "You didn't have to go through the dog and pony show of a royal wedding or a coronation."

"Stop complaining. You like being king. The only thing wrong with your job is there's no chance for promotion."

"I already have everything I want out of life," he said, kissing her sweetly.

They had no set itinerary. The yacht stopped wherever Morgan told it to. He and Suzanna went ashore at Portofino and Capri, and wandered through the winding streets hand in hand, stopping to look in shop windows like tourists. Sometimes at night they went to a local bar and socialized with the natives.

One day they anchored off Monaco and went swimming and snorkeling in the clear blue water. That night they got dressed up and dined in an elegant restaurant, then went gambling in the casinos.

At other times they had romantic candlelit dinners on the deck of the yacht under the stars, with music playing softly over the outdoor speakers. The table was always set with fine china and silver, and delicious food was served by waiters in spotless white jackets.

Afterward they made gloriously fulfilling love with moonlight streaming into the cabin, turning their tanned bodies to silver. It was a dream honeymoon come true.

By the time they started home, Suzanna felt like a new woman. She'd been under so much tension for so long. Now her taut nerves were completely relaxed. Morgan was always solicitous of her because of the baby, but she assured him, truthfully, that she felt wonderful as she began her new duties as queen.

Suzanna had wanted to finish her restoration work on the royal paintings. She had a proprietary feeling toward them by now. But she had to put her work on hold temporarily to appear at endless charity events and the state functions she was expected to attend. Suzanna rather enjoyed meeting all the people, but it was time-consuming.

"There's so much to do," she told Morgan.

"I didn't expect complaints so soon." His smile was a trifle forced.

"It's just that there's no time left over to spend in my studio. I like to finish what I start."

He pulled her onto his lap. "Cheer up, darling. As soon as we can announce that a baby is on the way, you'll be able to cut back on your engagements."

"It's too soon to say anything yet!" she exclaimed. "We don't want people to start counting the months and speculating."

"They'll be so thrilled that it won't even occur to them. But we don't have to make the announcement yet if you'd prefer not to." He stroked her flat stomach. "Nobody could ever tell you're pregnant."

"I feel great, too. I don't know why some women complain about the discomfort of having a baby. It's going to be a piece of cake!"

Suzanna was terribly upset when she got her period a few days later. She thought she was having a miscarriage. Knowing Morgan would be equally upset, she didn't tell him. If there was anything seriously wrong with her, she wanted to find out first so she could cushion the blow.

She made an appointment with a gynecologist, taking the precaution of using an assumed name and changing her appearance with a different hairstyle and nondescript clothes. Her ruse worked, because the nurse treated her like any other patient.

Dr. Roualt was calm and reassuring. "You're just

having your period. There isn't any evidence that you were pregnant.''

"But that can't be! I've always been irregular, but I've never skipped an entire month. I had all the symptoms, too. I felt like crying at the least provocation, I was tired but I didn't sleep well and I even felt sick some mornings.''

"A lot of things can cause a delayed period. Were you under any kind of stress?''

"Yes, a great deal,'' she admitted.

"There's your answer.'' The doctor smiled.

"That's hard to believe.''

"You can get another opinion if you like, but pregnancy—or the absence of it—is something even a first-year medical student can diagnose.''

"How could I imagine morning sickness?'' Suzanna asked skeptically.

"The mind can play tricks on the body. You thought you were pregnant, so your body supplied the symptoms. Extreme stress can affect a person in many ways. Believe me, my dear, your experience isn't unusual.''

"Then I *can* have children?''

"Without any doubt. Just try to relax and it will happen naturally.''

Suzanna left his office with mixed feelings—regret, but also a slight amount of relief. She'd been thrilled about having Morgan's baby, but he was naive to think there wouldn't have been speculation when the infant arrived in less than nine months. As long as she could have children, it was better that their first

one be conceived after the marriage, rather than before.

Still, Suzanna knew Morgan would be disappointed. She just wasn't prepared for his reaction. Instead of sharing her regret and planning for the future,
he simply stared at her with a frown on his handsome
face.

"How could you be mistaken about a thing like
that?"

She explained what the doctor had told her. "I was
under a tremendous amount of tension at that time,
with Jablon pressuring you to get rid of me and everything."

"It was touch and go there for a while, wasn't it?"
Morgan said with a slight drawl. "You couldn't be
sure who was going to win."

"I always had faith in you, darling," Suzanna protested. "But Jablon is devious. Those kind of people
are always dangerous."

"We were actually lucky that you got pregnant—
or thought you were. The timing couldn't have been
more fortuitous."

"I don't feel very lucky," she said soberly. "I really wanted the baby."

"Even though you forgot for days at a time that
you were pregnant?"

She frowned slightly. "I didn't realize that upset
you. I did have quite a few other things on my mind
at the time."

"Yes, I can imagine. But everything worked according to plan. Jablon's palace coup was averted, the

people of Monrovia accepted you and the wedding came off without a hitch.''

''You sound as if all those were bad things,'' she said slowly.

''Not at all. I admire you. There aren't many people that adept at getting what they want. Not even Jablon.'' Morgan smiled mirthlessly.

Suzanna had been confused by his cool, brittle manner. Suddenly everything became clear. ''You think I faked a pregnancy so you'd have to marry me!'' she exclaimed.

He didn't affirm the fact, but he didn't deny it, either. ''You must admit it was the catalyst for our marriage.''

''I told you that you didn't have to marry me!'' she flared. ''I didn't expect you to.''

''You knew I wouldn't abandon you at a time like that.''

Her eyes glittered with anger. ''You weren't so upset about the idea when it worked in your favor. Acquiring an instant family put a stop to any suggestion that you abdicate. *That's* why you married me, because I was suddenly useful!''

''That's the most twisted reasoning I ever heard,'' he said disgustedly. ''Did it ever occur to you that I wouldn't have been in that position if I hadn't refused to give you up?''

''You never asked me to marry you before I thought I was pregnant.''

''Because I thought you were dazzled by the idea of becoming a queen, without knowing what it entailed. And I was right. You're finding the duties tiresome already.''

The injustice of his suspicions outraged Suzanna. Her temper erupted like a volcano. ''You're just looking for excuses for your own behavior! You admit you think I married you for money and position. Well, you can have your jewels back.'' She tore off her engagement and wedding rings, along with a pearl bracelet and gold lion's head ring on her other hand. ''You can have your title back, too! You shouldn't have any trouble getting an annulment.'' The minute the words were out of her mouth, Suzanna was aghast, but it was too late.

Morgan's austere expression deepened. ''You don't mean that.''

It wasn't the response she was hoping for. It didn't tell her he loved her and couldn't imagine life without her. That was the way she felt about him. Tears threatened, but she was too proud to let him see them.

She held her head high and turned away. ''Do whatever you like. Just let me know.''

''Where are you going?'' he asked sharply.

''Does it matter?'' She left the room, walked through the apartment and out the front door.

Suzanna had no idea where to go or what to do. Her marriage had fallen apart in a matter of weeks, and she was alone in a foreign country. How had things gone so wrong, so fast?

It hadn't really been fast. Their problems went back a long way, but she hadn't been aware of them. Morgan had suspected from the first that she was like all his other women. He had overlooked the fact because of their awesome sexual attraction, but he was always on guard, looking for signs. She realized now what his mood swings had meant.

The question was, what was she going to do about the situation? Where was she even going to sleep that night? Certainly not in Morgan's bed! She could go back to her old room, but Suzanna knew what gossip *that* would start. Because it wouldn't be a secret for long.

Finally when she felt her emotions were under control, she marched back to Morgan's apartment. It was telling that she still thought of it that way.

He was standing motionless by the window, staring out at the garden with his back to the room. He turned around when he heard the door open. Joy flared in his eyes for a moment before Suzanna's grim expression registered. Then his face went blank and he remained where he was.

She tilted her chin defiantly to mask her vulnerability. "While we're deciding where to go from here, I'd like to have my own apartment. I presume that's one of the perks of being queen."

"I wouldn't want to cheat you out of any of your rewards," he answered ironically. "I'll have one of the servants prepare adequate quarters."

Suzanna's shoulders slumped in defeat. If Morgan wanted an annulment, she'd just have to live with it.

Chapter Ten

The atmosphere around the castle was chilly after Suzanna moved into her own apartment. She and Morgan avoided each other as much as possible. He'd given her an apartment almost as elegant as his, but more feminine, and he'd had the servants move over all her things. Each waited for the other to make the first move, and both were miserable when neither did.

Suzanna submerged her sorrow in work. She went to her studio every morning and tried not to think about what a mess her life had become. It worked to a limited extent, as long as she didn't have to see Morgan. The brief glimpses she had of him in the hall brought an almost unbearable yearning.

Unfortunately she couldn't avoid him completely. They were scheduled to appear together at the dedication of a new park. It was part of her royal duties. She was surprised that Morgan had time for such a minor event, but the curt note he sent her said the committee was expecting both of them.

If she didn't show up, people were bound to ask why, and how would Morgan explain it? Also, she didn't want to further his impression that she found her duties distasteful.

Suzanna wasn't sure Morgan would even notice, but she took extra pains with her appearance on the day of the dedication. She brushed her hair until it shone like a length of black satin, and made up her face carefully.

She might as well not have bothered. Morgan merely flicked a disinterested glance over her. Even with that autocratic look on his face, he looked so handsome that her heart gave a sudden leap. Suzanna could remember when those cool eyes had glowed amber with passion, and his chiseled mouth had brought her ecstasy.

"If you're ready, the car is waiting," Morgan said, bringing her back to reality.

Riding over in the limo together was awkward. They talked about the weather and commented that they were fortunate it was such a nice day for the dedication. When that subject was exhausted, Suzanna asked how long the ceremony would last—then regretted the question. It sounded as if she was anxious to get it over with. Which she was, but not for the reason Morgan supposed.

Finally he reached into his pocket, saying, "I think

you'd better wear these.'' In his extended palm were her engagement and wedding rings.

"Yes, I suppose you're right.'' She took them gingerly. "I'd forgotten about them.''

A muscle pulsed at his temple. "I know they're meaningless, but someone might notice that you don't have them on.''

"I didn't mean—''

"It doesn't matter,'' he broke in dismissively.

What's the use? Suzanna thought hopelessly. She hadn't meant the rings didn't matter to her, only that they'd slipped her mind, with everything else that was going on. But Morgan always thought the worst of her.

His attitude changed after they got to the park and people clustered around them. Morgan was suddenly transformed into an adoring husband. When people praised Suzanna's beauty and grace, he agreed and kissed her hand while looking at her adoringly.

That really hurt—the fact that he didn't mean it. She started to pull her hand away, but he held on and dipped his head toward hers.

"I know you hate to have me touch you,'' he murmured in her ear. "But we have to keep up appearances.''

Suzanna got through the dedication somehow. She even said a few words, which were well received. But by the end of the ceremony her nerves were in knots and her face felt stiff from the forced smile she'd worn for so long.

When they were finally free to leave, she hurried ahead of Morgan, taking the shortest way to the car by cutting across the grass. In her haste, she didn't see the gopher hole in the lawn. Morgan spanned the distance between them in two long strides, and caught her before she fell.

"You should have taken the path!" he scolded. "You're going to break your neck in those ridiculous heels."

"That would solve all your problems," she muttered, pulling away.

Morgan swore under his breath and let her go.

Suzanna didn't want him to know she'd twisted her ankle badly. She tried to walk normally, but her leg buckled.

With an impatient exclamation, Morgan swung her into his arms and carried her to the car. She had to endure the pain of being cradled in his arms without tenderness, and forced to appear unaffected by his potent male sexuality.

But when they arrived back at the castle the ordeal wasn't over. Morgan carried her upstairs to her suite—over Suzanna's vigorous protests.

"You can't even put your weight on that leg. How do you think you could get up all those steps?" He sat her on the edge of the bed and hunched down to examine her ankle. His hands were very gentle, in contrast to his curt manner. "It's not swollen yet, but we'll be able to tell more after your leg is X-rayed."

"That's ridiculous! You're making a big deal out of nothing. I just twisted my ankle, that's all. If I stay off it tonight, it will be fine in the morning."

"I'm calling the doctor. He'll be the judge of that. While we're waiting, you can get undressed."

As Morgan turned away, Suzanna stood and limped toward him. "I don't know why you're overreacting this way. I don't want to see a doctor, and I'm not going to get undressed."

"You'll do as I say, or I'll do it for you!" He scowled, gripping her shoulders. "I've undressed you before, and I can do it again."

Suzanna's anger was drowned by a wave of desire so fierce that she swayed toward him. Her lips parted and she said softly, "I remember."

Morgan's hands tightened as he examined her face for an instant. Then he gathered her in such a close embrace that their bodies were almost fused together.

"If you only knew how much I've missed you," he muttered, burying his face in her neck.

"You knew where I was," she said, clasping her arms around his waist and moving sensuously against him for the pure joy of it. "You could have walked down the hall."

"I didn't think you wanted me to. How could you have moved out and left me?" he asked reproachfully.

"I was terribly hurt. You accused me of some despicable things!"

Morgan smiled wryly. "I think we're even on that score."

Suzanna looked at him searchingly. "A marriage has to be based on trust, Morgan. Physical attraction isn't enough."

"Ours is pretty awesome!" The glint of humor in his eyes faded as he said quietly, "When you mentioned an annulment, the bottom dropped out of my world.''

''Mine, too. I said it in the heat of anger, but if you'd taken me up on it I would have been devastated.''

He lifted her in his arms and carried her toward the door.

She looked at him uncertainly. ''Where are we going?''

''Back where you belong,'' he answered deeply.

Suzanna's body was on fire with anticipation. As Morgan carried her down the hall to their apartment, she gave a bubbly little laugh. ''Let's drink a toast to royal duties. If we weren't obligated to appear at that ceremony today, we wouldn't be back together again.''

''You don't honestly think I usually go to those things?'' When she gave him a quizzical look, he said, ''I was so hungry for the sound of your voice that I called the committee and told them I wanted to be there with you.''

''They must have been thrilled,'' she said breathlessly as Morgan kicked the bedroom door shut and carried her to the bed.

''Not nearly as thrilled as I was when I could kiss your hand—even if you hated it.'' He set her on her feet and removed her jacket and skirt, then unzipped her lace shell.

''I was afraid you'd guess that I wanted you to kiss more than my hand,'' she said provocatively.

''My darling wife, I intend to kiss every exquisite

inch of you,'' he said huskily as he removed the rest of her clothes with tantalizing deliberateness.

Suzanna's desire mounted almost unbearably as Morgan flung off his clothes, then settled her gently on the bed and fulfilled his promise. She quivered as his warm, wet tongue circled her nipples and his hardened body gave proof of his own passion.

Their lovemaking that afternoon surpassed anything they'd experienced before. It was an apology for misjudging each other, and a reaffirmation of what they shared. Nothing was held back as they tried to bring more rapture than either had ever known.

In the calm aftermath, their hearts were still racing and their bodies were damp from spent passion. They clung together, utterly content.

Morgan had just enough energy to murmur, ''Promise you won't ever leave me again, my angel.''

''I promise,'' she whispered.

Even though Suzanna and Morgan were so grateful to be back together, things weren't quite the same. It was as though a tiny, almost imperceptible flaw had appeared in an exquisite piece of crystal. Or maybe she was just being insecure, Suzanna told herself.

Certainly Morgan was a doting husband. He begrudged the time they had to be apart. When she started going back to her studio every spare minute, he wasn't happy about it.

''You don't have to do that. I'll get someone else to take over the job,'' he said.

''I don't want you to. I told you, I like doing it,'' she answered.

"It takes too much of your time. How will you juggle working *and* a busy royal schedule? I'll never get to see you."

"I'll always have time for you," she said tenderly.

Morgan argued, but Suzanna managed to convince him that she could handle everything. She didn't tell him that she felt their marriage would be healthier if they gave each other some breathing space. She had to have her own interests.

He gradually accepted the situation. Morgan worked hard, too, but after a day of meetings, or being stuck behind a desk, he felt the need for some exercise. In the late afternoon he usually played tennis or went for a swim. And on the weekends he was especially active.

After Suzanna went back to work she didn't have time to join in Morgan's activities, but she wasn't leaving him in the lurch. He could always get a tennis game or find somebody to play racquetball with. Beaumaire Castle was the meeting place for his close friends.

At first, Morgan invited Suzanna along when he was going to the breeding farm to watch his racehorses exercise, or when somebody organized a tennis tournament. But after she turned him down a couple of times, he stopped asking.

They still spent their evenings together, so she didn't feel she was neglecting him. There were a lot of working wives in the world. The fact that she didn't have to work for a living wasn't really relevant, she told herself.

Suzanna gradually became aware of the fact that

Sophia was part of Morgan's inner circle. Actually, the redhead made sure that she knew about it. At parties they all attended, Sophia would seek Morgan out and make allusions to a tennis match they'd played, or some incident that involved the two of them.

At one gathering, Sophia was even more audacious. She made a date with Morgan right in front of Suzanna!

"Plan on having cocktails at my house after we come back from riding tomorrow," she told him. "I want your opinion of a new painting I bought."

"Thanks, but I won't be able to make it," he said. "Suzanna and I are going to the theater and there's an early curtain."

"You'll have plenty of time," Sophia assured him. "We'll have one quick drink while you look at the painting. I discovered a new artist and I want to know what you think of him."

Suzanna hid her anger and said to Morgan, "It's no problem, darling. I can always go with Kenneth and Alicia."

"I'm sorry, but it's impossible," he told Sophia. His face was expressionless as he glanced at Suzanna and added, "My wife and I spend little enough time together as it is."

Did Morgan think she didn't want to go with him? She only wanted reassurance that he wanted to be with *her!*

Someone called to Morgan and he excused himself and moved away, leaving the two women alone.

"It sounds like there's trouble in paradise." Sophia

gloated. Your marriage isn't as solid as you'd like me to think. Morgan knows he made a mistake.''

"I suppose you want me to think he told you that," Suzanna said scornfully.

"He's too much of a gentleman to do such a thing, but I can tell he isn't happy."

"It must be nice to be clairvoyant," Suzanna drawled.

"Don't think your marriage can't be dissolved," Sophia taunted. "Jablon would be delighted to find grounds for annulment. You're not in Morgan's class and you never will be. He should have married somebody with a title." As Suzanna opened her mouth to reply, Sophia left hurriedly, as usual.

That night while they were getting undressed, Suzanna looked for a way to bring up the subject of the other woman diplomatically. She didn't want to sound like a jealous wife.

"Sophia seemed quite disappointed that you wouldn't come for cocktails," she remarked casually.

"She'll get over it," Morgan answered dismissively.

"It almost sounded as if she was making a date with you," Suzanna said, gazing into the mirror as she brushed her hair.

"It wasn't a date. You could have come along if you wanted to." He took the brush out of her hand and started stroking it through her long hair.

"I wasn't invited."

"You're making a big deal out of nothing. You

heard Sophia. She has a painting she wants me to evaluate.''

"It's funny that she didn't think of asking *me*. That *is* my field.''

Morgan put down the brush. "This isn't a competition about who knows the most about art. She asked me because we're old friends.''

Suzanna realized they were on the brink of an argument. It would be prudent to drop the matter, but she couldn't. "Sophia seems to be here a lot. She's constantly referring to things you've done together, or are going to do.''

"We play tennis and other sports," he admitted. "But not just the two of us. The whole group is here just as frequently. You know all of them—Theo and Marcelle and Paulette, Kenneth, too, quite often.''

"Then you have plenty of other partners. Why do you need Sophia?''

"I don't need her," Morgan said with an edge to his voice. "But she likes to be with all of us, and I see no reason to arbitrarily exclude her from the group. You could come, too, if you wanted to.''

"That's a pretty lukewarm invitation.''

"It wasn't meant to be. You're welcome at any time. I've asked you repeatedly to share my leisure time, but you prefer to work," he said evenly. "You can scarcely begrudge me the companionship of my friends.''

"I didn't realize you thought of my work as dispensable," she answered stiffly. "I thought I was making a contribution to the country, something besides mere public appearances.''

Morgan's expression softened. "You *are* contributing, darling, and I'm proud of you. But I miss being with you." He took her in his arms and kissed her tenderly.

Suzanna put her arms around his waist and gave him a troubled look. "Nothing is more important to me than you, Morgan. Don't you know that?"

"It doesn't hurt to hear it once in a while," he said with a wry smile.

After they made love, all the sharp edges seemed smoothed over. But were they? Suzanna wasn't so sure, even curled up spoon fashion in Morgan's arms. Nothing had changed. Sophia was still very much in the picture. She spent more time with Morgan than Suzanna did! At least during the day.

There was only one way to protect her marriage. Starting tomorrow, the predatory redhead would have to find another tennis partner. The queen outranked her.

Morgan was surprised to find Suzanna still in bed the next morning. She was usually up and dressed by the time he arose. It was a long-standing habit of hers that was hard to break. She was used to having to commute to a job that started early.

"Don't you feel well, darling?" He looked at her with a frown of concern. "You're usually ready for work by now."

"I feel wonderful!" She sat up in bed and hugged her knees.

"Then why aren't you in your studio?"

"I thought we'd have breakfast together."

"Did you look at your calendar wrong? It isn't the weekend. Today is only Thursday."

Suzanna gave him a radiant smile. "Is there a law that says a husband and wife can't have breakfast together during the week?"

"If there is one, I'll have it rescinded." He ruffled her already tousled hair. "Do you know how sexy you look in the morning?"

"No, you'll have to tell me," she said demurely.

He kissed her bare shoulder above the sheet that covered the rest of her. "I'll tell you tonight." To her surprise, he threw back the covers and got out of bed. "Put on a robe while I call the kitchen and tell them to double my order."

He probably had a busy morning scheduled, Suzanna told herself, but she couldn't help feeling a twinge of uneasiness. Morgan had a healthy libido, and she was usually his first priority.

While they were having breakfast she said, as though she'd just thought of it, "It's such a gorgeous day. Why don't we play hooky and go someplace, just the two of us."

He raised a dark eyebrow. "Now I know there's something wrong with you. What happened to that rigid work ethic of yours?"

Suzanna realized she'd guessed right. Morgan did feel neglected. "I found out I'm not a superwoman. I can't juggle three jobs and give any of them the attention they deserve. I'd like you to look for somebody to finish the restoration work."

"Are you sure that's what you want?" he asked

slowly. "Or does this have something to do with our discussion last night?"

"Partly," she admitted. "It suddenly occurred to me that I'm passing up all the fun things in life out of a misplaced sense of duty. You're right about my work ethic."

"But you enjoy your work. I don't like to feel I pressured you into giving it up."

She thought he'd be delighted, not try to talk her out of her decision. "Don't you want me with you?" she asked bleakly.

He reached for her hand across the table. "My darling wife, I'd like to spend every waking moment with you! But I don't want you to feel obligated to do the things *I* enjoy."

"I enjoy them, too," she protested.

He looked slightly skeptical. "If you really mean it, I couldn't be happier."

"Would I ask you to get someone to finish the restoration if I didn't?"

That convinced him. "I'll tell Jacques to start looking today for somebody qualified," Morgan said enthusiastically.

Suzanna felt a small pang. It was like handing her cherished child over to a nanny. But that was nonsense. She would still oversee the work to make sure it was done right.

Giving him a bright smile, she said, "Now that that's settled, how about taking the day off to celebrate?"

"There's nothing I'd like better, but my schedule today is a killer. Some of the appointments were rescheduled from earlier in the week. I shouldn't cancel them again.''

At least that made her feel better. Morgan had a good reason for not dallying in bed this morning.

"How about meeting me at five o'clock?" he said. "We're having a tennis tournament."

"Can I be your partner?"

"You already are, darling," he answered warmly.

Suzanna worked in her studio that day, since Morgan was unavailable. The time flew by as always, and when she glanced at the clock in the late afternoon it was a quarter to five.

She flew back to the apartment and set a record for changing clothes. But still, by the time she got to the tennis court it was ten after the hour. Morgan and a group of other people were already there.

His face lit up when he saw her. "I thought perhaps you'd forgotten."

"Are you kidding?" Suzanna kissed him on the cheek. "I've been looking forward to this all day!"

Morgan put his arm around her shoulders and introduced her to the one person she didn't know, a very pretty young woman. "This is Marie, Marcelle's fiancée."

After the two women had exchanged pleasantries, Morgan said, "Since we have nine people now, you're promoted to line umpire, Sophia."

It was a logical decision, because all of the others were couples. Kenneth and Alicia were also engaged, and Paulette and Theo had been dating regularly. Sophia was the only one who was unattached.

She reacted to the "promotion" angrily. "I'm supposed to be your partner, Morgan! We've already played the semifinals. You can't change partners in the middle of a tournament."

"What's the big deal? This is scarcely Wimbledon," he said.

"That's not the point. We were ahead! You'll never win with *her!*" In her anger and frustration, Sophia got careless.

Morgan's expression chilled. "Are you referring to my wife?"

That pulled her up short. Sophia hastily tried to make amends. "I only meant that we have a chance to cream the opposition." She smiled nervously. "You'll never hear the end of it if you lose."

"I can live with it," he said curtly. Turning to the others, he said, "Shall we get started?"

Suzanna was an enthusiastic but indifferent tennis player. She played for fun, and wasn't devastated if she lost. That day, however, she really wanted to win.

Morgan excelled at tennis, as he did at all sports, and their opponents, Paulette and Theo, were almost equally good players. When Suzanna realized what she was up against, she tried too hard. Her body tensed and she missed shots she should have been able to return. Paulette and Theo's victory was never in doubt.

They would have won anyway, but Sophia's decisions didn't hurt them. Whenever there was the slightest doubt about one of Suzanna's returns, Sophia called the ball out.

Suzanna protested a couple of times and expected

Morgan to back her up, but he never disputed a call. He considered it bad sportsmanship.

When the match was over, Sophia rubbed salt in the wound. "Don't feel too badly," she told Suzanna with phony sympathy. "You don't play as much as the rest of us."

Suzanna gritted her teeth. "What you really mean is, I don't play as *well*. Isn't that it?"

"I wouldn't say that, but Morgan did win when I was his partner." Sophia laughed merrily.

"You did just fine, sweetheart," he said.

"Not really, but I wasn't as bad as Sophia made me look," she said defensively as the two of them walked off the court.

Suzanna decided to ignore Sophia and just enjoy herself. These gatherings really were fun. If only she could get rid of that objectionable woman!

That night, while she and Morgan were getting undressed, Suzanna brought up the subject obliquely.

"I had such a good time today," she told him. "I didn't know what I was missing all these weeks."

Morgan pulled his shirt out of his slacks and tossed it aside. "It was a treat for me," he said affectionately.

"You're just being polite. If you'd had Sophia for a partner you would have won."

"I did win." He parted her robe and kissed the cleft between her breasts. "You're my partner for life."

"That's sweet, but I don't want you to have to make excuses for me."

Morgan assured her that no excuses were necessary and ended the conversation with a kiss.

She hadn't accomplished much, Suzanna had to admit after Morgan fell asleep with his head pillowed on her breast. She didn't even get around to suggesting that it would be a lot healthier for Sophia if she found a gentleman friend. That had seemed a safe way to put it. Well, there would be other opportunities. She had no intention of giving up.

Suzanna was very upset when she discovered that Marcelle had organized a fox hunt for the next day. She didn't believe in killing animals for sport. Morgan felt the same way. She agreed to participate only after he explained that everybody just enjoyed the chase. The fox was allowed to go free at its conclusion.

The scene was very lively when Suzanna and Morgan got to the stables. Everyone was standing around talking and joking while the horses tossed their heads and stamped their feet. Grooms were busy saddling the guests' favorite mounts, and a young boy was trying to keep a pack of yelping hunting dogs under control.

Suzanna was uncomfortable when she saw how elegantly everyone was dressed. They were in fawn-colored jodhpurs and well-tailored dark jackets. She had on jeans and a blue mohair sweater over a cotton shirt because she hadn't been measured for riding clothes yet. They were all too well-bred to remark on the fact—everyone but Sophia.

She waited until she could get Suzanna alone. "Even *you* should know that's not proper attire. Poor

Morgan. You have absolutely no idea what's expected of a queen.''

Suzanna moved away without bothering to answer.

Morgan's horse was the magnificent black stallion he always rode, and the others had their own favorites. Sophia's horse was almost as powerful as Morgan's. *Wouldn't you know she'd be a good rider, also?* Suzanna thought disgustedly.

It was too bad the woman didn't have a personality to match her accomplishments. She heard Sophia asking which horse was Suzanna's, and then snickering at Molly, the placid tan mare.

In spite of Suzanna's reservations, the fox hunt turned out to be fun. It was a beautiful crisp morning and the foliage still glistened with dew. She liked the feeling of belonging as Morgan rode next to her and everybody called back and forth while they cantered through the woods.

Once the dogs flushed out a fox, the excitement level mounted. The fox was only a blur of red that the dogs had no chance of catching, but since that wasn't the goal, it didn't dim anybody's enthusiasm for the exercise.

At first Morgan hung back to stay with Suzanna, but she could tell he wanted to lead the pack. ''Go on ahead,'' she told him. ''Molly and I like to travel at our own pace.''

''If you're sure, darling.'' He took off after barely waiting for her assurance.

She watched indulgently as he galloped after the others. Morgan was sheer poetry in motion. He had perfect control over both his lithe body and the splendid horse. How was she ever lucky enough to marry this wonderful man? Considering the odds against their even meeting, it was a miracle!

As she trotted through the woods, happily reflecting on how blessed she was, Suzanna realized the sounds of the chase were getting fainter. She'd better stop dawdling and catch up or Morgan would worry about her.

Molly obediently broke into a gallop and the trees flashed by. Although Molly was docile, she was a trained hunter. She bunched her muscles and jumped competently over streams and low fences. Suzanna had never done this kind of riding before. Now she realized why Morgan found it so exhilarating.

By the time she caught up with them, the hunt was over. The fox had scrambled away safely and the dogs had been called off. Everyone was milling around a clearing in the woods. Molly leapt over one last fence to reach them.

Morgan saw her coming and raised an arm. When she raised her own arm to wave back, Suzanna felt something give way. Her saddle slipped to the right and her feet came out of the stirrups. She slid off the horse and fell to the ground. The breath was knocked out of her, but she fell on a bed of moss and pine needles.

Everyone shouted and immediately galloped toward her. Morgan reached her first, with Sophia right behind. He jumped off his horse and knelt beside her in one fluid movement.

"Lie still, darling." His face was very pale. "I'll send for a doctor."

"The poor little thing," Sophia said. She took off her jacket and put it under Suzanna's head. "You should have known she wasn't experienced enough to take those jumps, Morgan."

"You're right. It was criminally negligent of me!" he said in an agonized voice.

"You'll just have to realize she can't do all the things you like to do."

Suzanna finally got her breath back. "I didn't fall because I'm clumsy or incompetent. Something happened to my saddle." She tried to get up, but Morgan gently urged her shoulders down.

The others were now clustered around them. "I sent a groom back for a doctor," Kenneth said, looking at Suzanna in concern.

"I don't need a doctor." She struggled to sit up, pushing Morgan's hands away. "Look at my saddle if you don't believe me."

"We believe you, darling," he said soothingly.

"No, you don't." She stood and pushed through the circle around her to get to the saddle on the ground nearby. "There, look at that!" she said triumphantly. The leather cinch on the left side was ripped in two.

There were various exclamations, then they all discussed how such a thing could have happened.

"I intend to find out." Morgan's face was like a storm cloud. "I'll have the hide of whoever was responsible for this outrage!"

"I don't think any of the stable workers are to blame," Suzanna said evenly.

"She's right," Paulette said. "Those cinches get a lot of wear and tear."

"They should have been inspected," Morgan stated grimly.

"It's over and done with," Suzanna said. "The question now is, how am I going to get home? I don't feel up to riding bareback," she added with a faint smile.

"You'll ride with me." Morgan lifted her onto his saddle, then mounted behind her.

As they started back she said, "I sure know how to spoil a fun day, don't I?"

"Don't even think such a thing!" His arm tightened around her waist.

He was very solicitous. Suzanna had a hard time convincing him that she was only a little stiff and didn't need a doctor. After they returned to the castle, Morgan insisted on running a hot bath for her himself.

When he started to undress her, she said, "I want to talk to you about something first."

"It can wait until after your bath."

"No, I need to get this over with now." Suzanna took a deep breath. "I don't think what happened today was an accident. I think Sophia cut partway through the cinch strap on my saddle, knowing it would break when Molly took those jumps."

"Are you out of your mind?" Morgan was staring at her incredulously. "She was as concerned about you as the rest of us. She even took off her jacket and put it under your head!"

"Yes, that was a nice touch," Suzanna remarked ironically.

"I know you don't like Sophia, but you've made a shocking accusation."

"It's the truth," Suzanna said stubbornly. "And our dislike is mutual. Sophia is trying to break up our marriage."

"There was never anything serious between us," he said soothingly. "You have no reason to be jealous of her, darling. I'll admit she's tactless sometimes, but she'd never deliberately try to hurt anyone."

"How can you be so blind? I saw her standing near my horse before the hunt. She could have sabotaged the saddle. Your stable hands would never be that careless with the equipment."

"Then it must have been a defective strap."

"Why do you persist in defending her?" Suzanna exclaimed in frustration. "Can't you see she's trying to make me look like an outsider, somebody the rest of you have to make allowances for because I haven't had your advantages?"

"That's nonsense," Morgan said impatiently. "You're imagining things. Everybody loves you."

"Everybody except Sophia. If she really means nothing to you, I don't understand why you can't let her know she isn't welcome here. I gave up work I enjoy for *you.*"

He looked at her without expression. "I didn't realize it was quid pro quo. I thought you curtailed your hours because you wanted us to spend more time together."

"I did! I still do. But I also wanted to make you happy."

"So if I ban Sophia from the castle, that will make *you* happy?"

"Not when you put it that way."

"Just tell me what you want me to do, Suzanna," he said with restrained annoyance. "I'd like to have some peace around here."

"Do whatever you like. I don't care." She stalked into the bathroom and slammed the door.

The hot bath loosened Suzanna's taut muscles, but nothing could relieve the ache in her heart. Morgan thought she was being childish and petty. He couldn't see Sophia for what she really was, a spiteful, conniving woman who would do anything to get him back. The worst of it was, she was winning.

This argument with Morgan was serious. He was probably wondering why he'd ever coaxed Suzanna to join the group. She'd only participated twice, and both times she'd spoiled everybody's enjoyment. Everything had gone exactly as Sophia had planned.

But that was going to change. Suzanna's chin set grimly. Her marriage was the most important thing in her life. She didn't intend to let Sophia or anyone else destroy it.

Chapter Eleven

The next morning, Morgan suggested that Suzanna stay in bed that day, but she assured him that she felt fine. They were polite to each other and didn't refer to their argument, yet it was obvious that things weren't the same. They'd even gone to sleep on their own sides of the bed, not in each other's arms as they'd almost always done.

"Are we playing tennis or anything this afternoon?" Suzanna asked, determined to treat this as a normal day.

"No, I'm going to be tied up until dinnertime. You shouldn't exert yourself that much anyway, after your fall yesterday."

"I was only planning to watch, but it's just as well. The National Garden Association tea is today, and

I'm the guest of honor. I might not get home too early myself.''

''Well, have a nice day.'' Morgan pushed back his chair and came over to give her a kiss on the cheek.

They were acting like an old married couple, she thought bleakly as she went to get dressed.

Suzanna could have worked in her studio whenever she had some free time, but it had become a symbol of the discord between her and Morgan. So instead, she filled her days with royal duties. Requests for her to appear at various functions were always stacked up on her desk.

Gradually relations between herself and Morgan returned to normal, including their sex life. The chemistry between them was too potent to be ignored for long.

On the afternoons when the group got together, Suzanna always made it a point to be present. The first time, she'd steeled herself not to show any resentment toward Sophia, but the other woman wasn't there, not that day or the next time. It soon became clear that she wasn't part of the inner circle anymore. Suzanna would have been happier if Morgan had made the decision himself, without being prodded, but she resolved never to mention Sophia's name to him again.

Just when everything was running smoothly, another problem surfaced. Suzanna didn't feel well, but there wasn't anything specifically wrong with her. Mostly it was fatigue.

She was so tired all the time that it was an effort to fulfill her royal obligations and still keep up with Morgan. He had boundless energy and was always ready to party, even after a full work day. Suzanna had felt that way, too, until lately.

She didn't tell Morgan because he always overreacted and wanted to send for the doctor immediately. But she had no symptoms. Being tired wasn't an illness. It would sound as if she was trying to get out of her busy schedule. Then one morning the mystery was solved and Suzanna knew what was wrong with her. But how could she be pregnant? She'd been taking the same precautions as always.

Then Suzanna thought back to that terrible time when she and Morgan were barely speaking. She'd been so sure their marriage was over that it had seemed pointless to take her pills. When they'd made up so unexpectedly, she hadn't even thought about them.

Dr. Roualt confirmed Suzanna's suspicions after giving her a thorough examination. She'd once again donned her disguise and made the appointment under the same assumed name she'd used before. "Congratulations, my dear. I told you that you wouldn't have any trouble conceiving when the time came."

"Will I have any problem carrying the baby?" she asked anxiously. "I've been feeling really rotten lately."

"Morning sickness?"

She nodded. "And I sleep a lot, but I'm still tired."

"Those symptoms should go away shortly. I'll prescribe something to take for nausea, and some vitamin pills to supplement your diet. But from what I can tell, you're a very healthy young woman. Just eat sensibly, rest when you're tired and continue to live your life the way you normally do.''

''Can I exercise?''

''Yes, I recommend it—all things in moderation, of course.''

''How about tennis and horseback riding?'' she asked. He shook his head.

''I would avoid both of those. When I said to exercise, I was referring to swimming and long walks, things like that.'' The doctor wrote something on her chart, then looked up and smiled at her.

''I'll want to see you again in a few weeks. You can make an appointment at the front desk on your way out.''

Suzanna left the office filled with mixed emotions. Her own feelings were all positive. She was thrilled about the baby! The only question was, how would Morgan react? He might assume she'd stopping taking precautions without telling him—as he suspected the last time. Did he ever believe she'd honestly thought she was pregnant?

Their relationship had never been as trusting since then. How much damage would it cause if he thought she'd simply decided to have a baby without consulting him? Would he suspect her of another trick? A way to make sure he wouldn't leave her? It wasn't a secret she could keep forever. Morgan had to find out sooner or later. But perhaps it might be better if they discussed the subject first, so he'd feel part of the decision.

It was going to be a problem when she stopped

taking part in his strenuous activities. What excuse could she give, after clamoring to be included?

Oh, well, I'll think of something, Suzanna told herself. She was much too happy to worry about anything right now. If only she could tell Morgan—or at least *somebody!* Paulette and Alicia were both good friends, but she couldn't ask them to keep such a momentous secret. They wouldn't understand why it had to be a secret, and she didn't intend to go into her marital difficulties.

Her mother was the one Suzanna wanted to share the joyous news with, but she was afraid the older woman would start to worry. She'd had a difficult pregnancy the first time, and several miscarriages after that. It was the reason Suzanna was an only child.

By the time she reached home, Suzanna decided to call anyway. Her parents would be terribly hurt if they weren't told about their first grandchild right from the start, she assured herself as she dialed the phone.

Before she broke the news, Suzanna asked about her grandfather who had been sick.

"He's not doing well, I'm afraid." Mrs. Bentley sighed. "I'm really awfully concerned about him."

"Why didn't you tell me? Do you want me to come home?"

"No, don't do that! He isn't on the critical list, but he'll be sure he is if you come all that distance to see him."

"Is there anything I can do?" Suzanna asked.

"Just keep a good thought. The doctor says he's simply having a long, hard recovery, but you know what a worrier I am."

"Yes, I know." Suzanna smothered a sigh, realizing this wasn't the time to add to her mother's worries.

"I was hoping that you and Dad could come for a visit. I want you to meet Morgan."

"We're looking forward to it, but I'm afraid that will have to wait a little longer. But tell me about yourself. Are you making friends? Do you like living there?" Suzanna told her all the good parts about being married, her wonderful husband and how beautiful their apartment was. She talked about Paulette and Alicia, and Mrs. Bentley told her about friends at home.

"I guess Monrovia is your home now. It's hard to believe you're all grown up and married," her mother said.

"Didn't you get the wedding pictures?"

"Oh, yes, I meant to thank you. They were simply gorgeous! You looked like a little princess."

"Don't demote me, Mom, I'm a queen." Suzanna laughed.

"I loved your wedding gown, and your bridal bouquet and the tiara of flowers were exquisite. All the ladies at the charity guild said the same thing—all except that sour Eloise Bronson. She wanted to know where your crown was."

"I guess it's locked away in a vault somewhere. I've never had occasion to wear it," Suzanna said in an amused voice. "But Morgan has given me some gorgeous jewelry. Did you see my huge engagement ring, and the diamond necklace I was wearing? Point those out to Mrs. Bronson." She glanced up and waved at Morgan, who had come in and was standing motionless in the doorway.

"He's certainly a generous man," Mrs. Bentley remarked.

"Yes, I picked a real winner." Suzanna smiled at him. "Now, aren't you glad I didn't marry Steve Winslow?" she teased her mother.

They talked for a few minutes more. After she hung up, Suzanna went into the bedroom to look for Morgan. He had removed his tie and was unbuttoning his shirt.

"That was Mother on the phone," she said.

"I gathered as much. I didn't think you'd brag about your jewelry to a friend."

She frowned slightly at his tone of voice.

"We were only joking around. One of mother's friends wanted to know why I wasn't wearing a crown at our wedding. I told her to tell the woman about all the beautiful jewelry you've given me."

"Things Steve Winslow couldn't afford?"

"Good heavens, Morgan, I went with Steve in college! You can't be jealous of all my former boyfriends."

"I'm not jealous. I just wondered why you never married any of them. How I got so lucky, I mean," he added with a tight smile.

She didn't think that's what he meant. Not for the first time, Suzanna wondered if Morgan really believed she'd married him for what he could do for her. That made it easier to put off telling him about the baby. She wanted him to be as happy as she was, not look for ulterior motives.

* * *

That night they went to a party where Suzanna and Morgan both enjoyed themselves tremendously. By the time they returned home, their edgy little exchange before the party was forgotten. Their love-making that night was all either could have wished for. She cried out his name over and over again as he tantalized her with feathery caresses that made her long for his deeper touch.

"It's so wonderful to see you respond to me this way," he said, looking at her with blazing eyes. "Tell me I mean something to you."

"You're my whole world," she said simply, holding out her arms to him. "Don't you know that?"

Morgan gathered her close and kissed her almost frantically, urging their hips together until she was burningly aware of his hunger. Her own passion flamed out of control and she parted her legs and arched her body into his.

They rocketed into a world of sensation so intense that they writhed in ecstasy, uttering cries of joy. Morgan's driving masculinity carried them to ever greater heights. They reached the peak at the same time and called out each other's name in unison.

Even after the violent spasms subsided into gentle swells of satisfaction, Suzanna and Morgan remained joined together. It was the perfect time to tell him about the baby, but Morgan was drifting off to sleep and Suzanna's own eyelids were drooping. She'd tell him in the morning, she decided.

Morgan was gone by the time Suzanna awoke the next morning, and they kept missing each other all day. She was disappointed that her big news would now have to wait until after the embassy reception that evening. But that timing didn't work out, either.

When they returned home after the party, Morgan kissed her cheek and told her to go to bed, as he had work to do in his office that couldn't wait until morning.

Suzanna could have insisted that he come to bed instead, but that wasn't how she wanted to break the news. Something seemed to be telling her to keep her secret to herself, she thought somberly. Maybe the time just wasn't right yet. She had to convince Morgan that she loved him and only him, with all her heart.

Suzanna had to think up excuses for no longer participating in Morgan's strenuous activities. It taxed her ingenuity. She tried to solve the problem by accepting more royal speaking engagements, which meant she needed more clothes. That gave her another excuse—fittings with her dressmaker. She also told him there were notes that had to be answered and other official duties.

Eventually Morgan stopped asking her to join him at tennis or horseback riding or any of the other active sports he enjoyed. He seemed resigned to the situation. He continued to work hard and play hard, which suited his temperament.

Sometimes he didn't get back from playing squash or handball or whatever until quite late. Suzanna always asked about his day, but he didn't seem interested in sharing the details. One night she discovered why.

At a large reception she saw Sophia for the first time in weeks. Morgan's friends knew that relations were less than cordial between the two women, so Sophia wasn't invited to small, intimate gatherings. But this was a charity affair where anyone who contributed was welcome. Sophia lost no time in joining the group around the king and queen.

Suzanna decided to show Morgan she could be gracious. "I haven't seen you lately," she remarked to the other woman. "Have you been away?"

"No, I've been at the castle quite often," Sophia answered with a superior smile. "I guess you were busy doing other things." Suzanna felt as if she'd been shocked with a cattle prod. She glanced at Morgan, but he didn't seem flustered.

"I'll freshen your drink," Kenneth said hurriedly, reaching for her glass.

"What are you drinking?"

"Just ginger ale," Suzanna answered numbly.

"My goodness, you've given up *all* the fun things, haven't you?" Sophia laughed gaily. "I guess Morgan will just have to find somebody else to share them with."

He gave her a level look. "I can speak for myself— and I don't have any complaints."

It was too little and too late, Suzanna thought bitterly as she murmured a vague excuse and moved away with her head held high.

She and Morgan were both tense on the ride home,

but they were forced to make small talk because of the chauffeur.

The delayed argument exploded as soon as they reached their bedroom. "How could you make me such an object of ridicule?" Suzanna demanded. "Everybody there knew you've been seeing Sophia regularly. I guess that old saying is true—the wife *is* the last to know!"

"You're making a big deal out of nothing. Sophia has been here a few times—not as often as she led you to believe. I didn't mention it because it wasn't important."

"You know how I feel about her. *That's* why you didn't mention it."

He shrugged. "You're partially correct. This irrational jealousy of yours gets tiresome after a while."

"*My* jealousy!" Suzanna said furiously. "You were jealous of a man I went to college with—a boy, actually."

"The one who couldn't afford you?" Morgan drawled.

She ripped off her bracelet and threw it on the dressing table. "You can have your diamonds back! They're not worth what I have to put up with."

Morgan's face paled, but his stricken expression was gone in a flash. "So you admit you married me for the good life," he said evenly. "I suppose I should be glad that you're finally being honest with me."

"You're a fine one to talk about honesty," she said

scornfully. "At least I wasn't sneaking around, seeing someone behind your back."

"That's absurd! I wasn't keeping anything a secret. If you'd been interested in my company you would have known how I spent my time, and who my companions were. You made it clear that you wanted to go your own way. How can you object when I let you do it?"

"That's simply a good excuse for doing what *you* want!"

Morgan looked at her dispassionately. "Can you blame me?"

He didn't even bother to deny what was obvious— that he preferred being with Sophia. Suzanna felt a crushing sense of defeat, but pride prevented her from letting him see how deeply hurt she was.

"Since we're both getting what we want out of this relationship, I'll make it easy for you," she said coolly. "In the future you can come and go as you like without having to look for excuses."

His body tensed even more.

"What do you plan to do?"

"In the unlikely event that you need me for anything," she said ironically, "I'll be in my apartment."

Was that a look of relief on his face? She lifted her chin regally and left the room before her rigid control snapped.

Suzanna and Morgan had almost no contact with each other in the days that followed. If they needed to communicate they wrote notes and had them delivered by a servant.

Suzanna expected to hear momentarily that Morgan was seeking an annulment. What other solution was there to their problems when he clearly didn't love her anymore?

She was heartbroken over losing him. No man could ever take his place. But Suzanna had another problem. Should she tell Morgan she was pregnant? She was perfectly willing and able to take care of their child herself, but what if he wouldn't allow her to?

The child wouldn't be heir to the throne if their marriage was annulled. Could he still claim custody? Then she realized that Morgan could do whatever he wanted here. He was the king of Monrovia. His decisions were final.

The waiting and indecision were nerve-racking, but having to spend an evening with Morgan was worse. After days of silence between them, Suzanna received a note reminding her of a royal function they had to attend. This wasn't a maneuver on his part to be with her, like last time. The event had been on her calendar for weeks.

She dressed carefully for the evening, choosing a strapless red satin ball gown embroidered all over with small gold flowers centered by pearls. Instead of wearing her hair long and natural, she had it pulled back and styled in an elaborate cascade of waves and curls. Suzanna was determined to look her best. She wouldn't give Morgan the satisfaction of knowing how miserable she was.

She had to wear her engagement and wedding rings. Everybody would notice if they were missing. But as an act of defiance, she put on the long strand of imitation pearls she'd brought from home. That would tell him how little she cared about his jewels!

It was the only thing Morgan noticed when she joined him in the entry hall. Not her glamorous hairdo, or the beautiful gown that showed off her tiny waist and the curve of her breasts. Why had she bothered? Suzanna wondered hopelessly. Because of course she'd wanted him to think she looked beautiful.

"Where did you get those?" He looked at her pearls with a frown.

"You've seen them before. I wore them on our first date—although I wouldn't expect you to remember or be impressed. They aren't real," she added mockingly.

"Why aren't you wearing—" He stopped abruptly.

She knew he had almost asked why she wasn't wearing her diamond necklace, then remembered she'd left it in his bedroom. It seemed like a lifetime ago that they'd shared a bed.

"Shall we get this over with?" she asked curtly, walking toward the door.

"My sentiments exactly." Morgan followed and draped her satin cape around her. When his hand brushed her bare shoulder, they both jerked away. "Sorry," he muttered.

The evening was torture. They were forced to stand next to each other in a receiving line and pretend to be in love. It was even harder for Suzanna, knowing he was the only one pretending.

Morgan seemed to feel they weren't giving a convincing enough performance, so he put his arm around her waist while they were talking with a group of people later. The contact with his hard body made it difficult to mask her pain.

Finally Suzanna jerked away from him, saying she had to speak to someone. She walked away without looking back, so she didn't see his bleak expression.

In the limo on the way home, he stared straight ahead. His profile was austere in the dim light, but heart-wrenchingly handsome.

"I know what an ordeal these royal functions are for you, so you don't have to go to the Trade Alliance dinner on Friday. I'll make up some excuse for you."

"Morgan, I—"

He continued without letting her finish.

"You *will* have to be at the conclusion of the Grand Prix on Sunday, however. The king and queen are traditionally on hand to award the prizes. It would cause raised eyebrows if you didn't make an appearance."

"Morgan, we have to talk," Suzanna said wearily. She couldn't take much more of this, especially since it was only postponing the inevitable. Better to get it over with now.

But he refused to cooperate. "Not tonight, Su-

zanna. It's been a long day and I'm not in the mood
for recriminations.''

''I don't want to argue either, but I think we should
talk.''

''Not tonight,'' he repeated as the car pulled up to
the castle entrance.

Morgan didn't accompany her upstairs. He went in
the direction of the den and she went up to her rooms
alone.

Suzanna was drained of emotion by the time she
got undressed and climbed into bed. Maybe that was
just as well, because she had to make a decision, and
she couldn't let it be influenced by her feelings for
Morgan.

She had to leave Monrovia now, before the baby
was born. Morgan wouldn't stop her from leaving,
but he might prevent her from taking the baby if she
waited until it was born.

When the decision was finally made, Suzanna felt
almost a sense of relief. The pain would return later,
but the feeling of hopelessness and turmoil were over.
On Sunday night after the Grand Prix she would tell
Morgan she was leaving.

Suzanna used the rest of the week to tie up loose
ends. She spent time supervising the work in her studio, as she'd done intermittently since turning the job
over to the man Morgan had found to take her place.
He was quite capable and the restoration process was
all but finished, so she wasn't abdicating her professional responsibility.

One day that week she had a last lunch with Alicia. Suzanna explained that her grandfather was ill, and she was planning to return home for a visit, which was true. She merely neglected to mention that she didn't intend to return.

Her last chore was to sort through her clothes. All of the beautiful ball gowns and couturier-designed dresses went into one closet, along with their coordinated accessories. Those things she would leave behind. She was taking home only what she'd brought with her—except for a baby and a broken heart.

Suzanna dressed casually for the Grand Prix in a simple yet elegant tweed suit and a white silk shirt. It was an appropriate outfit for a sporting event. There was nothing sexy about it except for the short skirt. But Suzanna had given up trying to attract Morgan's attention.

The conclusion of the race would take place at a luxury hotel near the castle. Officials and timekeepers with stopwatches and flags stood expectantly at the finish line, making sure the large, enthusiastic crowd stayed off the road. Morgan and his entourage watched from inside the royal enclave, a roped-off section of lawn in front of the hotel.

As soon as they arrived, he and Suzanna went in separate directions, by unspoken agreement. If they didn't stay together, they didn't have to keep up appearances. Morgan was surrounded by his friends in the middle of the lawn, and Suzanna joined a different group near the road where the cars would appear shortly.

She found that if she smiled a lot and looked interested, she didn't have to say much. People were flattered by her apparent attention. Actually, Suzanna's eyes kept wandering to Morgan.

He looked especially regal in a superbly tailored navy jacket and white flannels. His silk shirt was open at the neck and he wore an ascot instead of a tie. At least one of them was having a good time, Suzanna thought bitterly. White teeth gleamed in Morgan's tanned face as he laughed at someone's comment.

She turned away hurriedly, but a few moments later she couldn't resist glancing in his direction again. There would be so few opportunities left and this was a good way to remember him. Not austere, or even passionate, but carefree, the way he'd been the first time she saw him. Finally, to hang on to her composure, Suzanna had to concentrate her attention on her companions.

Morgan watched her covertly. He was aware of everybody she talked to, every graceful movement she made. His attention was so focused on Suzanna that the changed mood of the crowd didn't register at first. They'd been cheering excitedly as the first cars began to appear. Now there was a hum of apprehension as a car approached with smoke pouring from its engine.

Morgan glanced at the road as the car went out of control and swerved directly toward the people gathered near the road.

He shouted a warning to Suzanna, but she didn't hear him because of the noise. While he watched in horror, the car headed straight for the spot where she was standing. None of the group was paying attention to the road.

Morgan acted instinctively. He raced over, grabbed her and dragged her out of the way. The others scattered and the car miraculously missed them and careened across the lawn until it was stopped by a tree.

Everything happened so quickly that Suzanna didn't quite grasp what had occurred. She was drawing back to look at Morgan when Jablon appeared out of the crowd and roughly pushed her aside. His only concern was for the king. Suzanna was caught off balance, with nothing to grab on to. She landed hard on a gravel path.

Morgan was down on his knees beside her in an instant. He turned her over and drew in his breath sharply. Her eyes were closed and blood was dripping from a cut on her forehead where she'd landed on a rock. "Get an ambulance here immediately!" he ordered before bending over her again. "You have to be all right, my love," he pleaded in a hoarse voice. "I wouldn't want to live without you. Please don't leave me." When she opened her eyes, he exclaimed, "Thank God!" He gathered her in his arms and held her fiercely.

It felt so wonderful that Suzanna thought she had died and gone to heaven. She sighed and closed her eyes again.

"Are you in great pain?" he asked anxiously. Before she could answer, Jablon bent over them.

"Were you hurt, Your Majesty?" he asked.

"How dare you put your hands on the queen?"

Morgan thundered. His fury was barely contained. "If you know what's good for you, you'll leave us alone. I'll deal with you later," he added ominously.

Everything became very confused from then on. The ambulance arrived and Morgan rode with Suzanna to the hospital where doctors and nurses hovered over her.

The cut on her head required several stitches and Morgan insisted on holding her hand during the procedure.

"Don't worry," the doctor told Suzanna. "You won't even have a scar."

"I want you to do a complete X ray to find out if she has any broken bones," Morgan ordered.

"That won't be necessary, Your Highness. We did a thorough examination. The queen is just fine except for that cut and a couple of bruises on her knees."

Suzanna was concerned about more than a few bruises. She'd worried about the baby all the way to the hospital. "Doctor," she said hesitantly, giving Morgan a covert glance, "is there any chance that I could be damaged internally?"

He smiled reassuringly. "You were just shaken up, not seriously injured, fortunately. Don't worry, the baby is fine." He turned to Morgan. "I won't say anything, of course, until you're ready to make the announcement, Your Highness."

As the man left the room, Morgan stared incredulously at Suzanna.

"You're pregnant?" He looked torn between joy

and outrage. "Why didn't you tell me? How could you let me find out this way?"

"I didn't know if you'd be pleased," she answered simply.

"You didn't think I'd want our child? The precious life we made together out of love?"

"I didn't think you loved me. It didn't seem to bother you that we were practically not speaking after that bitter quarrel. You wouldn't even discuss it."

"I was afraid you were going to tell me you were leaving me. I thought if I could prevent you from saying it, somehow we'd work things out."

"I thought you wanted your freedom," she said. "When you didn't come near me, I assumed you were arranging an annulment."

"How could I give up the love of my life?" He took her hand and kissed the palm tenderly.

"My worst nightmare came true when you told me our marriage hadn't lived up to your expectations, and then moved out of our bedroom."

"You didn't act like you cared," she said wistfully.

"Are you serious? I was so desperate to touch you that I put my arm around your waist when you couldn't object. You can't imagine how much it hurt when you jerked away."

"Oh, Morgan." Suzanna laughed helplessly. "How could two people who love each other have so many misunderstandings?"

"I don't know, but that's all behind us." He smoothed her hair and kissed her lips very gently.

"I've missed you so, darling. When you're feeling better I'm going to show you just how much."

"I can't wait that long." She held out her arms to him. He looked at her doubtfully.

"I don't want to hurt you, sweetheart. I love you too much."

She smiled enchantingly. "The only thing you have to avoid is my forehead, and I think we can both live with that. Could you please find the doctor and tell him I want to go home to my own bed?"

Morgan's eyes took on the special glow she remembered so well. "That's a good idea, my love," he said in a velvet voice. "And I think you should stay in bed for at least a couple of days."

"That's what I was counting on," she answered softly.

Epilogue

Kenneth's wedding to Alicia had been cause for celebration throughout the country. But the event most eagerly awaited had been the birth of the future monarch of Monrovia. The entire population had counted down the days of Suzanna's ninth month.

"You thought nobody would notice if our baby was born a little early," she teased Morgan. "Now aren't you glad the first time was a false alarm?"

"I'm thankful for everything since you came into my life," he answered adoringly.

Suzanna gazed fondly at the little cherub in her arms. "I might be a tiny bit prejudiced, but I'd say this is one sensational-looking baby."

"Positively regal," Morgan agreed with mock solemnity.

Prince Alaine Gerard Emile de Souverain had an impressive name, but the future king of Monrovia looked anything but regal at the moment. The rosy-cheeked infant was clutching his father's finger with a dimpled hand while chortling happily.

"The people are crazy about him," Suzanna said complacently. "Gifts have been pouring in. Even Jablon sent a silver cup with Alaine's name engraved on it."

Any mention of his ex-minister brought a scowl to Morgan's handsome face. "He's lucky I didn't have him thrown in jail for assault after what he did to you! In addition to all of his other transgressions."

"You're really just an old softy," Suzanna said affectionately. "It was nice of you to find a place for him on the Commodity Pricing Board."

Morgan laughed unwillingly. "Those people are so contentious they won't even notice how abrasive Jablon is. He'll fit right in."

"Don't try to minimize the gesture. It was a very generous thing to do."

He shrugged. "Jablon served the monarchy well before he got old and overzealous. I couldn't just turn him out to pasture. He wouldn't know what to do with himself."

"I think his gift to the baby shows he appreciates your tolerance."

"Speaking of gifts, I have something for you."

"Not another present!" she exclaimed. "I already have everything I could possibly want."

"Wait here, I'll be right back."

It was still hard to believe sometimes that all of

their problems were now just distant memories, Suzanna reflected as she placed the baby in his crib. Jablon was out of their lives and so was Sophia. Suzanna couldn't quite forgive the other woman for all the trouble she'd caused, but it was hard not to feel sorry for her. After Morgan ordered her, in no uncertain terms, to stay out of their lives, Sophia was so angry and frustrated that she went to live in France. Well, maybe she'd be happier there, Suzanna thought.

Morgan returned carrying two beautifully wrapped boxes.

"*Two* presents?" Suzanna exclaimed.

"Well, actually, one is for Junior, here." Morgan handed her the smaller of the two boxes. "I don't think he'll mind if you open it for him."

She started to chuckle after she'd untied the ribbons and removed the lid. Inside was a miniature golden crown. When she propped up the baby and put the crown on his head, it slipped to one side. His wide grin added to the comical effect. The crown prince of Monrovia looked like a mischievous little imp.

"He's going to make a great king." Morgan gazed at his son with pride. "He won't take himself too seriously."

"He's lucky to have someone like you as a role model," Suzanna said softly.

Morgan kissed her lovingly, then handed her the second box. "Now open your present."

Inside was a small treasure chest. It was enameled in royal blue and gold, with Suzanna's monogram on top outlined in small diamonds.

"It's gorgeous, Morgan!" she gasped. After examining the exquisite workmanship, she said, "But you've given me so much jewelry that it won't all fit in here."

"Those are only material things. You've given me more than I could ever give you—our beautiful son."

Suzanna's eyes were misty as she lifted the lid. Inside the box was a strand of opera-length pearls, each one perfectly matched and glowing with an inner light. They were so luminous that anyone could tell they were genuine.

"These are fabulous!" she exclaimed. "I've always wanted real pearls. How can I ever thank you, darling?"

"Just promise you'll never leave me," he said in a husky voice.

"I don't need any incentive to promise that." She wound her arms around his neck. "You'd be the king of my world if we lived in a one-room apartment and had to scrounge around for the rent."

"I'd still be the richest man alive if I had you, my love," he answered deeply.

The kiss they exchanged expressed the depth of their feeling, a love that would bind them together for the rest of their lives.

* * * * *

Look for Tracy Sinclair's heartwarming love story as she returns to Silhouette Romance in summer 2000 to join their 20th Anniversary celebration.

MONTANA Mavericks™

Return to Whitehorn

*Look for these bold new stories set in
beloved Whitehorn, Montana!*

CINDERELLA'S BIG SKY GROOM by Christine Rimmer
On sale October 1999 (Special Edition #1280)
A prim schoolteacher pretends an engagement
to the town's most confirmed bachelor!

A MONTANA MAVERICKS CHRISTMAS
On sale November 1999 (Special Edition #1286)
A two-in-one volume containing
two brand-new stories:

"Married in Whitehorn" by Susan Mallery
and
"Born in Whitehorn" by Karen Hughes

A FAMILY HOMECOMING by Laurie Paige
On sale December 1999 (Special Edition #1292)
A father returns home to guard his wife and child—
and finds his heart once more.

*Don't miss these books, only from
Silhouette Special Edition.*

Look for the next **MONTANA MAVERICKS** tale, by
Jackie Merritt, on sale in Special Edition May 2000.
And get ready for
MONTANA MAVERICKS: Wed in Whitehorn,
a new twelve-book series coming from Silhouette Books
on sale June 2000!

Available at your favorite retail outlet.

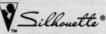

Silhouette®

TM
Visit us at www.romance.net

SSEMAV

Looking For More Romance?

Visit Romance.net

Check in daily for these and other exciting features:

Hot off the press

View all current titles, and purchase them on-line.

What do the stars have in store for you?

Horoscope

Hot deals

Exclusive offers available only at Romance.net

Plus, don't miss our interactive quizzes, contests and bonus gifts.

PWEB

Of all the unforgettable families created by
#1 *New York Times* bestselling author

NORA ROBERTS

the Donovans are the most extraordinary. For, along with
their irresistible appeal, they've inherited some rather
remarkable gifts from their Celtic ancestors.

Coming in November 1999

THE DONOVAN LEGACY

3 full-length novels in one special volume:

CAPTIVATED: Hardheaded skeptic Nash Kirkland has *always*
kept his feelings in check, until he falls under the bewitching
spell of mysterious Morgana Donovan.

ENTRANCED: Desperate to find a missing child, detective
Mary Ellen Sutherland dubiously enlists beguiling
Sebastian Donovan's aid and discovers his uncommon abilities
include a talent for seduction.

CHARMED: Enigmatic healer Anastasia Donovan would do
anything to save the life of handsome Boone Sawyer's
daughter, even if it means revealing her secret to the man
who'd stolen her heart.

Also in November 1999 from Silhouette Intimate Moments

ENCHANTED

Lovely, guileless Rowan Murray is drawn to darkly enigmatic
Liam Donovan with a power she's never imagined possible. But
before Liam can give Rowan his love, he must first reveal to
her his incredible secret.

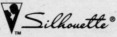

Silhouette ®

Available at your favorite retail outlet.

Look us up on-line at: http://www.romance.net

PSNRDLR

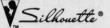

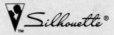

THE FORTUNES OF TEXAS

*Membership in this family has
its privileges...and its price.
But what a fortune can't buy,
a true-bred Texas love is sure to bring!*

Coming in November 1999...

Expecting...
In Texas
by

MARIE
FERRARELLA

Wrangler Cruz Perez's night of passion with Savannah Clark
had left the beauty pregnant with his child. Cruz's cowboy
code of honor demanded he do right by the expectant
mother, but could he convince Savannah—and himself—
that his offer of marriage was inspired by true love?

THE FORTUNES OF TEXAS continues with
A Willing Wife by Jackie Merritt,
available in December 1999 from
Silhouette Books.

Available at your favorite retail outlet.

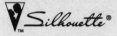

Silhouette®

Silhouette®

SPECIAL EDITION

COMING NEXT MONTH